KNIGHTS in a BAR ROOM
NORMA
WINDY CITY KITTY
Lilas
Marie
Sadie
THE POWERS GIRL
"Nobody's Baby"
"HELL'S BELLE"
gunmoll 2nd
"SKY WITCH"
PRETTY BABY
Crosby's Curse
NOT IN STOCK
HELLZAPOPPIN
CHANGE O' LUCK
"BABY"
JOLTIN' JANIE
PETE the CARRIER

The JOLLY ROGERS

The BEST DAMN HEAVY BOMBER UNIT in the WORLD

The JOLLY ROGERS

Southwest Pacific 1942-1944

Schiffer Military History
Atglen, PA

EDITORIAL STAFF

Supervision

Captain Bernard E. Stoecklein

Editor

Master Sgt. Jules F. Segal

Art Editor

Staff Sgt. Leonard H. Baer

Photo Editor

Staff Sgt. Joseph Silvering

Library of Congress Catalog Number: 96-72652.

Printed in China.
ISBN: 0-7643-0258-2

We are interested in hearing from authors with book ideas on related topics.

Published by Schiffer Publishing Ltd.
77 Lower Valley Road
Atglen, PA 19310
Phone: (610) 593-1777
FAX: (610) 593-2002
E-mail: Schifferbk@aol.com.
Please write for a free catalog.
This book may be purchased from the publisher.
Please include $2.95 postage.
Try your bookstore first.

ACKNOWLEDGEMENTS

S/Sgt. Charles B. Ingram and S/Sgt. Lewis L. Bergman, for much of the source material in ***Odyssey of The Jolly Rogers.*** ★ 2nd Lt. Charles F. Horne and S/Sgt. Donald Magness, for invaluable assistance in business management of this book. ★ Capt. F. A. McLaughlin, Lt. Lovejoy, and ***Jolly Rogers*** Photo Section, for their splendid cooperation and selection of photographs. ★ ***Yank Down Under,*** for reproduction rights to cartoons and photographs.

And the following photographic sources, to whom indebtedness is gratefully acknowledged:—S/Sgt. Gerald R. Minder; S/Sgt. A. V. Panetta; S/Sgt. J. R. Helbert; T/Sgt. Stephen J. Novak; T/Sgt. John A. Boiteau; S/Sgt. William De Rue; S/Sgt. Dan Capriola; S/Sgt. Robert C. Wurster; S/Sgt. Francis Martin; S/Sgt. Dan Hentscher; S/Sgt. Ted C. Jackson; S/Sgt. William Metaxotos; S/Sgt. Willard D. Erbeck; S/Sgt. Richard B. Crook; S/Sgt. John M. Salek; Captain Bill De Jarnett; Captain Joe Black; Myron C. Davis (Life Magazine); Sgt. Dick Hanley (Yank Down Under Magazine); Ken's Men Photo Section; Head Hunters Fighter Squadron; Far East Air Forces Photo Section.

A bow also to Len Segal, whose editorial assistance in the production of this book was indispensable.

TABLE OF CONTENTS

Lt. General Kenney says:-

"It's only natural that the Jolly Rogers are part of the best damn Air Force in the world. With the kind of support the Jolly Rogers have given us, we'll give the Japs the best damn licking in the world."

Maj. General Whitehead says:-

"The Jolly Rogers have what it takes . . . and they've given it to the Japs, with interest. When the war history of the South West Pacific is written, one of the brightest chapters will be yours. My congratulations to a top-rank outfit, known from Suez to Singapore."

Ennis C Whitehead
Maj Gen USA

Brig. Gen. Crabb says:-

At the

"According to newspaper and magazine stories, people don't know whether Fifth Air Force is part of the Jolly Rogers Air Force or the Jolly Rogers part of the Fifth Air Force. Seriously, I'm proud of your bombing record — as proud as you yourselves are. When bigger and better bombs are dropped on bigger and better targets . . . . the Jolly Rogers will drop 'em."

J. V. Crabb

HELM OF THE

Lt. Col. E. W. Scott, Jr.

Lt. Col. Robert J. Colleran.

Lt. Col. A. C. McDonald.

"As one who has been in the South West Pacific Area for a long period of time, I can truthfully say that there are few heavy bomber units who have contributed so much to the success of our campaigns against the enemy. I am proud to be your new Chief. I congratulate all of you, whether your job is on the ground or in the air, on your contribution to the work that has made the Jolly Rogers the famous war machine it is today."

Lt Col. A.C

"The Jolly Rogers have remembered Pearl Harbour in a way the Japs will never forget. Flier or cook, mechanic or clerk, you've done the job you were sent here to do, and done it superbly. Praising the Jolly Rogers is like carrying coals to Newcastle, so I will simply say that I am proud to have taken part in the battle beside you."

Col. Carl A. Brandt.

Lt. Col. Harry J. Bullis.

Col. Ralph E. Koon.

Brig. General Ramey

Col. Arthur H. Rogers.

Hall of Fame

ODYSSEY of the JOLLY ROGERS

1. American Chapter

Activated at Key Field, Mississippi, April 15, 1942, the *Jolly Rogers*, as they were later to become known, had no planes or pilots, and consisted of a cadre of two officers and 73 enlisted men. The ground crews, having no equipment, spent their time drilling. One month later, they were transferred to Barksdale Field, La., Shangri-La of Army Air Bases.

The wheels began to turn. LB-30's flew in, later followed by Consolidated B-24 Liberators. Personnel streamed in. Combat men from all over the United States reported for duty. Pilots from Randolph and Kelly Fields. Air mechanics from Shepherd Field, Tex. Armorers from Lowry Field, Denver, Colo. Gunners from Las Vegas, N.M. Clerks from Fort Logan, Colo. Radio Operators from Chanute Field, Ill.

At the helm of the *Jolly Rogers* were Lt. Col. Eugene P. Mussett, Capt. Robert B. Savage, 1st Lt. A. C. McDonald. Staff Officers were Major Marion D. Unruh, 2nd Lt. Samuel E. Lumpkin, 1st Lt. George Wilson, Capt. James King, 2nd Lt. Roger Lindsey, 2nd Lt. James McAnally, 2nd Lt. Lee Petty.

Unit flight leaders were Captain Pattison, later succeeded by 1st Lt. Roy L. Taylor; Major Arthur H. Rogers, later to become one of the most distinguished figures of the *Jolly Rogers*; Major Margrave; Captain Delbert Hahn; and Captain Harry J. Bullis, another future top man.

The men of the *Jolly Rogers*, most of whom spoke with the drawl of Dixie, were teachers, toolmakers, students, surgeons, wool salesmen, engineers, accountants, editors, draftsmen, lawyers, coaches, linesmen, farmers, ball players, missionaries. Out of this crazy quilt of civilian backgrounds, Barksdale Field training forged the beginnings of the professional Air Corps Jap steamroller.

The next move was to Greenville, S.C. The two B-24's of the advance echelon were the first bombers ever to land on the Greenville runway. Because of the widely dispersed areas of the airfield (just in case), the standing joke of the day was getting a three-day pass from one unit to visit a friend in another.

More personnel from Air Force schools, including the first navigators and bombardiers, joined the *Jolly Rogers* at Greenville, during intensive flight training and cross-country hops. Here we acquired "Ace" Dunmore, and swapped twenty undersized pilots for twenty six-footers. Then the aerial gypsies moved again to Henry Ford's Willow Run Bomber plant at Ypsilanti, Mich. Goal of the Willow Run Plant — one complete B-24 every hour.

The men who were to fly and maintain these huge airbirds trained beside the workers who built them. The EM's all lived, slept, and worked in one vast hangar. More personnel flocked into the *Jolly Rogers*, to be greeted by Major Rogers' brusque query, "What the hell can *you* do?" Key officers who signed in were 1st Lt. Roger B. Keeney, Capt. Robert S. Holt, 1st Lt. Roy Dye, Capt. William Doeller; 1st Lt. Taylor relieved Captain Hahn.

Two weeks at Willow Run, and the *Jolly Rogers* went westward ho, on trains travelling four different routes, leaving the air echelon behind temporarily. At California's Camp Stoneman, the rumors started flying as campaigns for Government insurance policy and pay allotment began. New items of clothing and equipment were issued. Then pistols and rifles, which were choked in cosmoline, taking two days to clean. Slings were put on upside down, the hangar was bathed in grease, and the ordnance inspection resembled a Keystone comedy.

In a week, everything was loaded and ready to go. Wearing full field equipment and carrying their barracks bags, the *Jolly Rogers* filed up the gangplank on board a transport so sea-weary it had carried American troops to battlefronts in another war twenty-five years before. On September 4th, 1942, the *Jolly Rogers* were officially overseas.

2. Pacific Chapter

There was only one submarine scare. After occupying themselves on board with K.P., guard duty, draw poker, dice, and sea-gazing, the *Jolly Rogers* heaved a sigh of relief when Oahu's brown and green mountain crests appeared on the horizon. War-planes wheeled overhead as

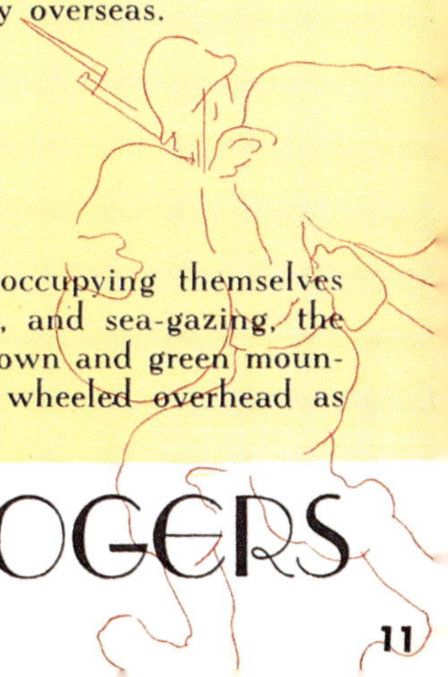

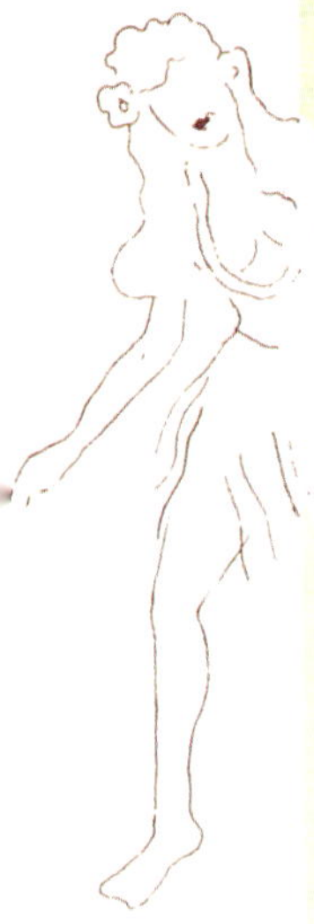

they steamed into Honolulu Harbor, docking under the camouflaged Aloha Tower. A welcoming band whooped it up with "Song of the Islands."

A ride on the Oahu Railway "pineapple express" wheezed them to Hickam Field, nine miles from the port. Some of the *Jolly Rogers* landed in the huge central barracks, still a shambles from Pearl Harbor Day. Others drew four-man bungalows beneath palms at Hickam Field; cottages at Wheeler Field; a cane field at Kipapa, enlivened by red mud and red dust; and the opposite coast of the island, Kahuka. The Chairborne Division of the *Jolly Rogers* had to make the best of a cottage and a two-story stucco apartment house with refrigerators, private tile showers, electric stoves and fans . . . fifteen minutes from Honolulu.

A few days later groundmen watched admiringly as a perfect formation of fourteen *Jolly Rogers* Liberators flew in from Diamond Head, completing in a dozen hours what it had taken the seafarers eight days to do. The rest followed shortly, and that day Col. Ramey succeeded Lt. Col. Mussett as top man. Combat training was resumed in earnest—in the grim atmosphere of the birthplace of our war with Japan. Helmets and gas masks were carried even off the posts. No lights showed after dark. Hickam Field still showed shattered hangar roofs, bullet-riddled barracks, filled-in bomb craters. Barbed wire and bomb shelters were everywhere.

Bombardiers practised laying eggs on towed sea-sled targets. Pilots and combat crews flew armed reconnaissance missions over the Islands. Ground crews tackled maintenance work with growing enthusiasm. The time was coming. . . .

Off duty, however, the *Jolly Rogers* made the most of what they yet might spend. At Honolulu, the Pali, Waikiki Beach, they learned the meaning of words like *wahine, Pau, Pilikia,* and *hoomalimali.* Despite the discouraging odds of 187 men for every woman on Oahu, *Jolly Rogers* Casanovas could be seen on the prowl in remote corners of the island. When game was snared, the snow would fall thick and fast. At last, bloated with pineapple juice, fed up with the woman and liquor shortage, the *JR's* were not unhappy to learn that Australia was the next stop. Never were crates and boxes conceived and dedicated with such enthusiasm.

Before leaving Hawaii, several changes were effected. Top man Colonel Ramey was succeeded by Colonel Meehan. Lt. Col. Unruh left for greener pastures, was replaced by Lt. Col. Rogers.

On October 29, 30, and November 1, 1942, the air echelon took off from Hickam Field. Making stops at several South Pacific bases, the echelon reached Ipswich, near Brisbane, Australia, on schedule, without losing a plane on the 5,000 mile hop. On November 7th, the remainder of the *Jolly Rogers* boarded a new Norwegian transport, one that had been at sea when the Quisling Government took over, and had reported at an English port for service under the Norwegian Government-in-exile.

Joining a convoy with war escort, the transport sailed westward. On November 11th, at 11 a.m., the troops stood in ranks on deck while "Taps" were blown. The following day the convoy crossed the Equator. Initiations into the Ancient and Honorable Order of Shellbacks were made at the Court of Neptune Rex, complete with "kangaroo court" and sentences of extremely messy punishment for hapless victims. Guns were fired during the celebration.

On November 16th, when land was sighted, the Captain of the ship was presented with a surprise contribution of about $1,100 by the troops, for the relief of the families of Norwegian sailors. As he thanked them over the P.A. system, the convoy sailed into the Fiji Islands.

Next morning a curtailed convoy continued across the International Date Line, hopelessly confusing everybody. On November 25th, having made its way north through the Great Barrier Reef, our transport landed at Townsville Harbor, reminiscent of Southern California or Old Mexico. Shortly afterward, bare-legged Aussies on shore were throwing up Australian coins in exchange for American coins and cigarettes. The *Jolly Rogers* were down under.

3. Australian Chapter

American trucks trundled the men to a transient camp some miles from town, where they spread their equipment on open ground shaded only by the great, white-trunked gum trees of Australia. The first fresh water showers in three weeks were instantly jammed. Changing uniforms, about half the men went into town for their first contact with Australians. Some lucky individuals found themselves overnight hotel space — beds with sheets and mattresses!

On the afternoon of the next day the *Jolly Rogers* climbed aboard the trucks again, driving back to the docks. They sat on their barracks bags until the sky was clear and star-studded, with a bright full moon, waiting to go up another gangplank. Then, in the quiet of the night, a blood-curdling sound — the air raid siren! The war had become reality.

They did not break ranks until ordered to seek shelter. Dock lights went out, the town blacked out. Soldiers ran between speeding bikes and lorries hurrying away from the port. Most of the men stayed beside the sea wall, waiting. Fifteen minutes later, at the "All Clear," steel helmets came off. Some of the boys, anxious for their first taste of the "McCoy," were disappointed.

Long after midnight the last man was counted aboard, and the troops curled up on the deck and the floor of the hold, the only sleeping accommodations. They were under way by noon. Long lines formed aboard for mess and latrine needs, and water was scarce. Three days and nights of this, the worst if shortest voyage of all. Anchor was finally dropped off the eastern coast of Cape York Peninsula. Troops were landed by barges.

Then an eighteen-mile dusty trip through dense jungle to a new camp area ideal for Tarzan and his mate, but somewhat discouraging to the *Jolly Rogers*, especially since gas, bombs and food were the shipping priorities, in that order . . . and the third priority seldom arrived. The air echelon had beaten them there for several weeks, and had already been in active combat. They had met the Zero, and he was theirs. First Zero for the *Jolly Rogers* (and for any B-24 in the SWPA) had been scored by S/Sgt. Clifford McCarthy on November 15, 1942. Major Harry Bullis had sunk a Jap cruiser in Rabaul Harbor with two direct hits.

Colonel Ralph E. Koon was now top man of the *Jolly Rogers*. His flight leaders were Major Phillip J. Kuhl, Major Roy L. Taylor, Major Cecil L. Faulkner, and Major Bullis. 1st Lt. Roger Lindsey found his services in great demand, and all sections of the *Jolly Rogers* began to put into practise what they had learned in the last seven months.

The Medics more than once risked their lives in attempts to save crews from flaming wreckage. The Chaplain, Captain William Beeby, provided an EFM Wireless Service, so that the *JR's* could remember those back home on sentimental occasions. The boys handling bombs and maintaining planes kept on the hop as B-24's roared back and forth between Aussie and Jap Island bases northward.

During this period an outbreak of artistry and baptism took place, with the christening of *Dirty Gertie*, *Ain'tcha Sorry*, *Yanks From Hell*, *Eager Beaver* and *Liberty Belle*. The end-papers of this book show what this fad started.

Combat-wise, the *Jolly Rogers* decided to save time and increase striking range by sending a unit at a time to operate from Port Moresby. For six weeks the outfit operated from the Northern Territory, with one advance prong always in New Guinea.

During this time they were already making history. On January 8, 1943, pilots Taylor, Gottke, Campbell, Andrews, Hesse, Sayre, Almond and Wilson pounced on the Lae enemy convoy. A large transport and many barges were sunk. Eight out of twenty-one Nip air attackers were scuttled, and all our B-24's came home looking like sieves, thanks to ack-ack and 20 mm. explosive fire.

On January 20, 1943, five B-24's flown by Major Faulkner, Lt. Dowie, Lt. Cook, Lt. Shaffer and Lt. Olsen, roared over Wewak seeking an enemy convoy. Instead they found 25 Zeros overhead. Outnumbered five to one, they dropped from nine to two thousand feet, but the Nip hornets followed. One after another the B-24's were hit and damaged, but each was protected by others. The Nips paid for their attack with twelve definitely destroyed, six damaged. Each *Jolly Rogers* bomber collected holes, came home safely, and no casualties.

Another brilliant bit was contributed by Lt. Lark Martin and Lt. Paul Johnson, searching for a missing Liberator. They sighted a five-ship convoy approaching Wewak and shadowed it. Eighteen Zekes objected, pressing home fierce attacks down the coast to Nubia, then inland to Bena Bena. During the unequal two-hour engagement in which five men were wounded, none fatally, Lt. Martin's plane was limping on two engines, covered by Lt. Johnson. The two crews collected six Zeke scalps, four probables. A flying sieve with 400 holes, Lt. Martin's ship landed on one good tire, which blew out on touching the strip. Lt. Johnson's Liberator was almost as badly battered.

To tell all the heroic stories of the *Jolly Rogers* would require two books like this with no pictures. But mention in this chapter of their history should be made of some of the unforgettable heroes of the outfit, such as Lt. Norman D. Smith, sole survivor of a sea crash, who spent nine days on a life raft and 28 days in a trek through New Guinea jungles to rejoin the *Jolly Rogers*.

There was Captain Charles E. Jones, zooming his *Dirty Gertie* into a formation of Zeros, scattering the Japs, shooting down the Nips' leading ace, earning the hatred of Radio Tokyo, which boasted *Dirty Gertie* had been destroyed. (Ain't so, Tokyo.) Captain Jones then succeeded Major Kuhl as flight leader. And Lt. Hank Chovanec, whose *Falcon* had sunk more ships than any other B-24 in the *Jolly Rogers*, conducting a personal grudge fight with Nippon, for good reasons of his own.

There was S/Sgt. Grady Gaston, who spent 141 days in the Northern Territory jungles after a crack-up, living on snakes, fish and crocodiles, and losing 60 pounds in weight before being rescued. And Captain Holt, who didn't have to, but flew as observer, gunner, bombardier, even pilot *pro tem*, and was finally lost in action over Lae. A man to remember.

Our Lt. Col. Scott, at that time with "Ken's Men," scored the still unbeaten SWPA bombing record of eight enemy boats sunk. Captain Foskett, later *JR* Adjutant, won his wings flying over enemy targets, one of the few ground men in the theatre to win this unique honor.

By the time the *Jolly Rogers* were ready for the dragon-shaped isle of New Guinea, there were 29 vessels less in the Jap Navy, and 91 Zeros less in the Jap Air Force, courtesy this outfit alone. But the best was yet to come.

4. New Guinea Chapter

On February 10, 1943, all units of the *Jolly Rogers* with the exception of one which spent six months at Darwin, were stationed at Port Moresby, New Guinea. Not too long afterward, the Japs welcomed the *Jolly Rogers* with their famous one hundred plane raid on Moresby, one of the biggest Nip raids since Pearl Harbor.

On March 1st, Lt. Higgins was flying a recco north of New Britain when he caught the first sight of an enemy convoy that was shortly to become headline news all over the world. Twenty-two Jap ships, heading south-west towards Lae — the famous Bismark Sea Convoy. Some *Jolly Roger* planes joined the all-out force of B-17's, B-24's, B-25's and A-20's, escorted by Beaufighters, P-40's, P-39's and P-38's, that attacked the convoy for three days. The Bismark Sea battle ended with 15,000 Jap troops killed, 22 enemy ships sunk, 54 enemy planes shot down, with as many more damaged or probably destroyed. Allied cost—only five planes. Not one Jap ship reached Lae.

A brilliant piece of recco work was scored by 1st Lt. Ceylon H. Brainard on March 30, 1943. He spotted four Jap destroyers, radioed their position to our naval forces, then snapped doggedly at their fleeing heels despite the barrage of flak thrown up at him. During his sleuthing Oscars jumped him three times. First a formation of eight (one exploded, one flamed, one dived smoking); then six (one hit); then six more. The crew's guns went out during the third attack, so Brainard called it a day and took his pock-marked bomber home after five hours of relentless shadowing. Eleven Silver Stars, by order of Gen. Kenney.

On July 8, 1943, the Darwin-based unit of the *Jolly Rogers* rejoined the family at Moresby. They had been having some fun on their own. Inspired by the symbol of co-pilot and ex-Disney cartoonist Lt. Ken Strong's creation, *Asterperious* (definition: "A superior attitude in an

inferior environment"), they had done an *asterperious* job on the Japs themselves.

Sweeping over the Dutch East Indies sector (Sourabaya, Bali, Macassar, Celebes, Manokwari, Ambon,) they had sunk eleven ships, damaged four, scared hell out of a lot more. In five months of operation they had battled their way through 208 Jap interceptors, sometimes against odds of 7 to 1. The ten-hour missions were too long for top-cover, so they fought their own battles. Gunners accounted for 45 definites, 11 probables, 3 damaged. Combat cost—one man killed, four wounded, apart from the tragic loss of Capt. Olsen (who succeeded Capt. Jones) and his ace crew, through being rammed during the long-range raid on Macassar by a suiciding Jap float plane. The *Asterperians* produced two genuine aces—S/Sgt. William C. Simon and S/Sgt. George Rice.

Three days after the *Asterperians* returned to the fold, Col. Arthur H. Rogers became the new boss-man, with Lt.-Col. Bullis next in line. Col. Rogers, a man of exceptional dash and color, led the *Jolly Rogers* through General MacArthur's aerial blitz war that culminated in the utter defeat of the Japs in Guinea and New Britain.

The *Jolly Rogers* paid their first daylight visit to Wewak on August 8, 1943, warming up our enemies with some huge oil and warehouse blazes. Five Zekes got in the way—three licked their wounds. Eleven days later the *Jolly Rogers* went back again in sunlight, plastered oil dumps once more. Thirty Zekes intercepted—thirteen received aerial burial, seven probably joined them.

Fifty Wewak enemy fighters challenged a formation of six *Jolly Rogers* on September 15. The whole base rocked with glee when our planes returned, well-ventilated, but with the scalps of 27 definites, 5 probables and 3 damaged. Only one of our airmen was wounded.

Perhaps the most historic and highly publicised mission of the *Jolly Rogers* was the first daylight raid on the Jap fortress of Rabaul. Against a wall of flak and fierce interception, the *Jolly Rogers* won a lion's share of glory for the day. "Ace" Dunmore bombed himself into headlines and a Sydney leave when the flight he led sunk a destroyer and a submarine, and severely crippled a large destroyer tender and another sub, with one run over the target. This despite a forty-minute attack by forty to fifty enemy fighters, eight of which bit the dust, four probably, and six were damaged.

Another unit smashed dock installations and warehouses, dunked one tub, damaged another. We lost one plane, which was mercilessly strafed into the sea by five Zekes. This unit accounted for six kills.

On December 20, 1943, Lt. Col. Bullis received the sceptre of the *Jolly Rogers* from Col. Rogers, and Maj. Charles Preston Whitlock was appointed his deputy. On February 21, 1944, in the midst of heavy air operations against Cape Gloucester, Saidor and Arawe, the *Jolly Rogers* left Port Moresby for Dobodura. The move was something of an achievement, considering that it was made while our bombers were kept flying without let-up.

Four days later Maj. Roy Taylor led a six-ship strike against enemy shipping in Hansa Bay at 7,500 ft. Japs on land and sea filled the sky with lead, but two large cargo vessels disappeared into wreckage, debris and oil slicks. Sixteen angry Zekes came up, seven of which promptly went down; but not *via* a three-point.

On this same day, Maj. Gottke flew a beautiful unarmed recc mission over Jap territory, 500 miles north-west of Truk. On the way u he had to fly on instruments for two hours at 1,200 feet until daybreal Despite the fact that his plane was entirely alone over a strong enemy ai base, more than a thousand miles from friendly territory, he made thre leisurely runs over the target to get an adequate number of photograph Gottke and his crew brought home the first American snaps of thi important Jap island group. And did it using the only navigation map available—Russian naval charts dated 1828.

We almost claimed a P-47 on March 8, 1944, when our B-24 attacked Awar drome and were jumped by seven enemy fighters. Twent minutes later, after two Zekes had been blown out of the skies, P-47 showed up unexpectedly. Our gunners' training in aerial recognitio undoubtedly saved their necks.

Another move . . . and the *Jolly Rogers* on the ground were again bu making the new camp home-like. Among the improvements made we a daily ice-cream cone, a P.A. system on the way, a malted milk ba "hot" kitchens on wheels for the ground crews doing night work at t strips. This last idea was the innovation of Col. Carl A. Brandt, wh succeeded Lt. Col. Bullis on March 18th, with Lt. Col. Edward W. Sco Jr., as his assistant.

At this stage of *Jolly Roger* history, the Army's rotation poli suddenly moved out of the rumor class, and some of our old-timers wav farewell to their tent-mates, who didn't believe it either.

On March 30, 1944, the *Jolly Rogers* were part of the first big Fi Air Force daylight smash at Hollandia. On this mission, "Ace" Du more's flight again won glory by dropping their eggs smack in the cen of eighty to ninety planes on the ground. Other units of the *Jolly Roge* started huge, cheery fires all over the base.

It is impossible in this short space to narrate all the great feats of su pilots as Maj. Whitlock, Lt. Crawford, Lt. Chevonec, Capt. McWillian Maj. Paul E. ("Buzzin' Johnny") Johnson, Capt. Shaffer, and dozens other famous *Jolly Roger* names. But their deeds will never be forgott by the crews who fought with them, and the ground men who work beside them.

Our story closes with the assumption of leadership of the *Jolly Rog* by Lt. Col. Scott, with Lt. Col. Robert J. Colleran as deputy, in June, 19 But the story of the *Jolly Rogers*, in actuality, is still going on.

FLASH! As this part of the book went to press, word arrived o strictly *Jolly Rogers* show over the Palau Islands on June 10, 1944, o of the most magnificent in our history. A medium force of unescorted Liberators took off in miserable weather to bomb Peleliu Airdrome, o a few of which failed to reach the target. From forty to fifty Zek Oscars, Hamps and Tojos intercepted—but viciously. In the 38-mini scrap we destroyed twenty of the enemy definitely, eight probably, a damaged three. Our losses were amazingly slight.

The *JR's* bombs blew up ammo dumps, burned hangars and inst lations. Fires and explosions covered the entire airfield area. An indefin number of aircraft were destroyed on the ground. Peleliu is, at t moment of writing, an important enemy drome in the SWPA.

"I wonder if it isn't about time we replaced Sergeant Campbell."

—Courtesy of YANK Down Under

"Listen, Roger, I don't care if you are a first-class navigator —don't refer to me as your relief-map!"

AT HOME IN THE Jungle

Northern Territory—Jolly Rogers' first SWPA camp.

Wooden it?

Subsidiary, General Electric, Inc.

GI Club House, GI-built.

Roll out the gun-barrel.

Eastman Kodak, Markham Valley

Stork Club, Port Moresby. Chairs are made of bomb fin crates.

Radio City Music Hall. No, that little house is the projection booth.

Peanuts, ice cream, razor blades, gum drops . .

Form 81-BVD, in quadruplicate, gets you a nail.

Parachute rigger. If it doesn't open, bring it back.

They came, they sawed, they constructed.

Sunday at Doba Dura.

Aerial view of JR's camp in Markham Valley.

Autumn in Port Moresby.

Roadway.

*B*e it ever so humble, there's no place like the jungle — so we made it like home. We built sites where nothing stood before, then tore them down almost as soon as they were finished. The world will little note, nor long remember what we did here, but the natives will never forget what we built here.

The latest thing in foxholes.

At home.

Wine — precious as gold.

The house of tomorrow.

Water — precious as wine

Fifth Avenue.

MOVING

M-DAY . . .

We've packed just about everything but the fuzzy wuzzies. You're telling *us* we're the best-equipped Army in the world! Praise the Lord and pass the spinach. Or a spare set of muscles.

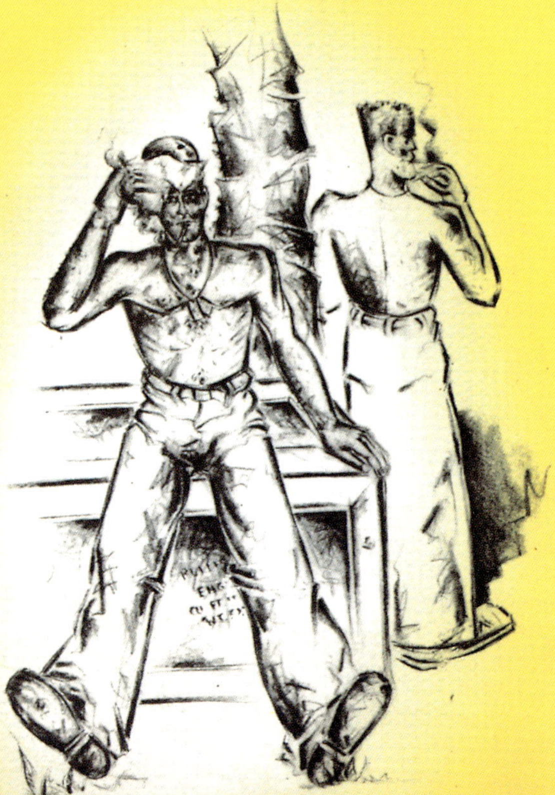

GOODBY TO ALL THAT . . .

All that we just finished building, we mean. Jungle-wise GI's start packing the moment the last nail gets hammered in our old camp. Muscle conservation plan: half the guys put up the camp while the other half tear it down.

BUSINESS AS USUAL . . .

While the new camp goes up, combat man keep going up also. The only thing dustier than a new runway is a Hoover campaign button. Ashes to ashes, dust to dust; if mud don't get ya, Guinea dust must.

—Ain't It Hell, Boys?

DIG, DIG, DIG, WELL ALL RIGHT

Aussies aren't the only diggers in the SWPA. But the new camp's gotta go up, so our shovels go down. Pity to distoib the woims, ain't it? Just the sympathy one woim feels for another.

WRING OUT THE OLD...

Moving doesn't leave you smelling like this spring's geraniums. So after a day's digging, the day's washing begins. Dear, dear, tattletale gray? Gray, hell—it's broadcast black! Cigar courtesy Christmas parcel mailed one year ago.

DEAR JOE...

"...You lucky stiff! Wish I was there fighting the Japs beside you. Things are tough at home—can't get any gas for weekend trips, steak is rationed, and as for taxes! But we're keeping a stiff upper lip, digger..."

"LOAD 'EM UP—WE'RE GOING!"

The word comes . . . the bomb trucks jounce out. You can do twenty mph if you want to . . . but with a coupla thousand pounds of hot stuff behind you — would *you?*

Nice fresh eggs today. No rationing here!

Tin fish need fins, for land or sea.

It's on wheels . . . but it still ain t feathers!

"Midnight Mechanics" do their stuff. Night loading is an old story with *JR* groundlings. Remember when "getting loaded tonight" meant something else?

Courtesy of YANK Down Under

"But don't you remember *anything* about last night?"

"It's those size 13 canal boats of his!"

Into the Wil

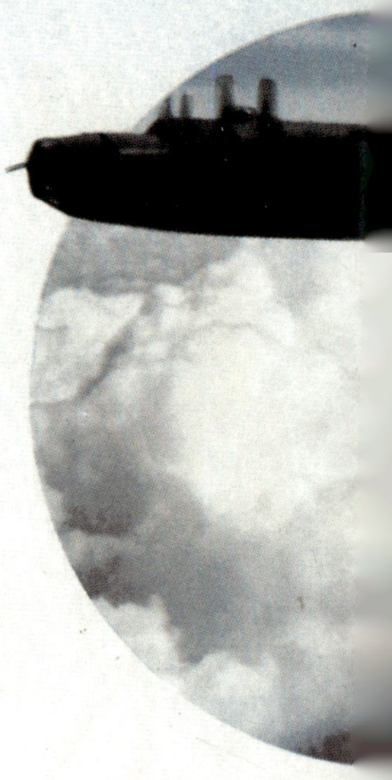

Blue Yonder . . .

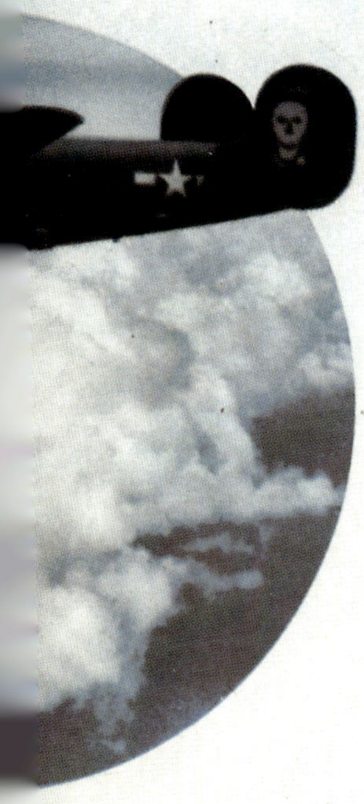

Above fantastic mountain caps,
To reach the lair of hated Japs,
The five-nosed dragons fly.
The crews are ready at each gun,
The bombs are ready, ton on ton . . .
Now will you shout "Banzai!"?

Now will you gloat and will you strut
And will your chin so proudly jut,
And will you boast of winning?
Will you find it consolation
To realise your devastation
Is only just beginning?

AITAPE
BEFORE

AFTER

260,000 TONS

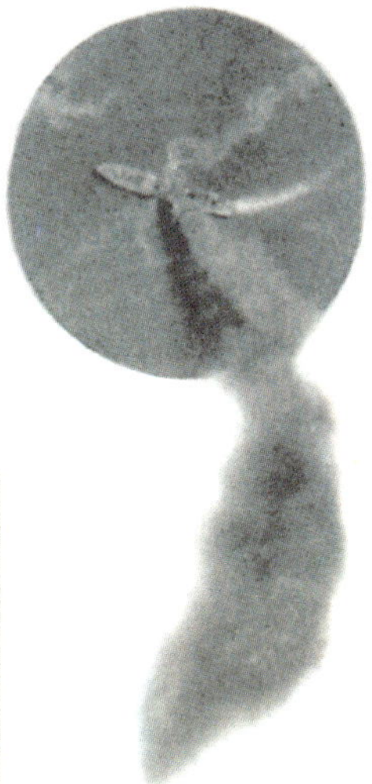

Sunk

NOTE: These particular photographs represent ships sunk by Fifth Air Force Bombers of all classifications, and are used solely as atmosphere for these pages, owing to the difficulties of obtaining good close-up shots of ship bombings by heavy bombers.

Skip-bombing

Damaged
116,000
TONS

Look out— Below!

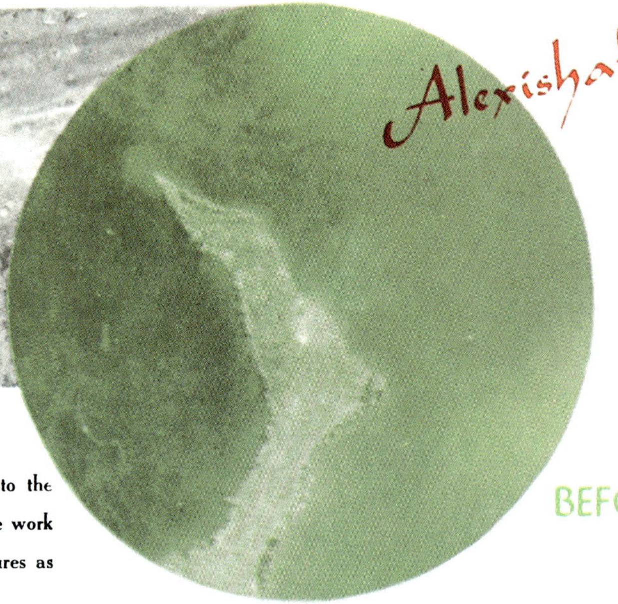

"FINE WORK." On completion of the Jolly Rogers strike against Peleliu Airdrome at Palau, V Bomber Command's Brig. General Crabb wrote:— "The attached pictures are evidence of good work on the part of your personnel. I know that such good bombing is only the result of fine maintenance and fine organization on the part of all personnel assigned to the unit. I wish to congratulate you and all of your personnel on the fine work you have done." And General Crabb marked the two bombing pictures as below:—

Makassar
Dagua
Hollandia
AFTER
Biak Island
Rabaul

Ancestor —Courtesy

374
DEFINITES

More scrap iron for Japan only it's their own, this time Figures for Jap planes shot down do not include hundreds of enemy aircraft destroyed or damaged on the ground by bombing.

Bound
Jolly Rogers!

The spectacular record of the **Jolly Rogers** *in shooting down enemy fighters is the result of one thing—intensive gunnery training on the ground. This is accomplished in part through giving all crews constant practice on a skeet range.*

120
PROBABLES

89
DAMAGED

ONE . . .

WO !

NOTE: Photos on these two pages were taken by automatic cameras in the noses of medium bombers and fighters. Heavy bombers have no mechanical apparatus for photographing enemy planes shot down.

PRESIDENTIAL CITATION

GENERAL ORDERS
NO. 21

WAR DEPARTMENT
Washington, May 6, 1943.

Extract

IV.—Citation of units in the United States Forces in Southwest Pacific Area. As authorized by Executive Order No. 9075 (sec. III, Bull. 11, W.D., 1942), citation in the name of the President of the United States, as public evidence of deserved honour and distinction, was awarded to the following-named forces. The citation is as follows:—

THE *Papuan Forces, United States Army, Southwest Pacific Area,* are cited for outstanding performance of duty in action during the period July 23, 1942, to January 23, 1943. When a bold and aggressive enemy invaded Papua in strength, the combined action of ground and air units of these forces, in association with Allied units, checked the hostile advance, drove the enemy back to the sea-coast and, in a series of actions against a highly organized defensive zone, utterly destroyed him. Ground combat forces, operating over roadless, jungle-covered mountains and swamps, demonstrated their courage and resourcefulness in closing with an enemy who took every advantage of the nearly impassable terrain. Air Forces, by repeatedly attacking the enemy ground forces and installations, by destroying his convoys attempting reinforcement and supply, and by transporting ground forces and supplies to areas for which land routes were nonexistent and sea routes slow and hazardous, made possible the success of the ground operations. Service units, operating far forward of their normal positions and at times in advance of ground combat elements, built landing fields in the jungle, established and operated supply points, and provided for the hospitalization and evacuation of the wounded and sick. The courage, spirit and devotion to duty of all elements of the command made possible the complete victory attained.

By order of the Secretary of War:

G. C. Marshall
Chief of Staff.

OFFICIAL:
J. A. ULIO,
Major General,
The Adjutant General.

—Courtesy of YANK Down Under

"Oh, brother, gander those wicked looking power turrets!"

"Oh, they're just some of my Jolly Roger pin-up boys."

SACKTIME SPECIALISTS

A HORIZONTAL gallery of unfortunate combat fatigue cases, all recipients of the D.S.C. (Distinguished Sacktime Cross.) The Shuteye Squad is shown here in typical afternoon manœuvres. Positions adopted are those prescribed in "Army Training Manual Z-Z-Z-1." Intrepid warriors all, these *Jolly Rogers* have slept through earthquakes, storms, work call and chow call. Their fighting motto: "A Nap a day keeps the Nips away."

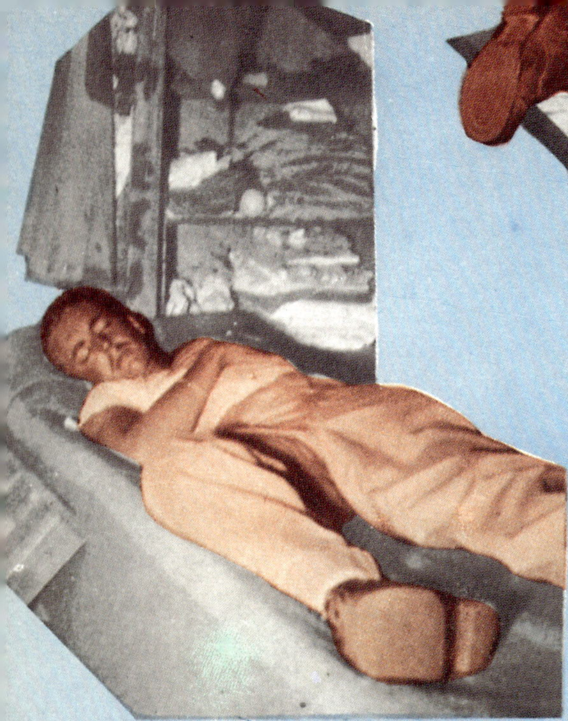

The horizontal bicycle spread.

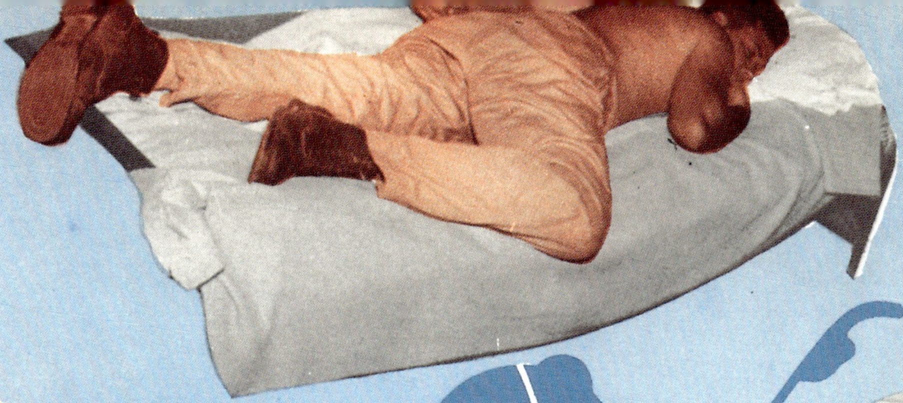

The combination belly plunge and thumb-suck.

The elevated knee twist.

The R.I.P. recline.

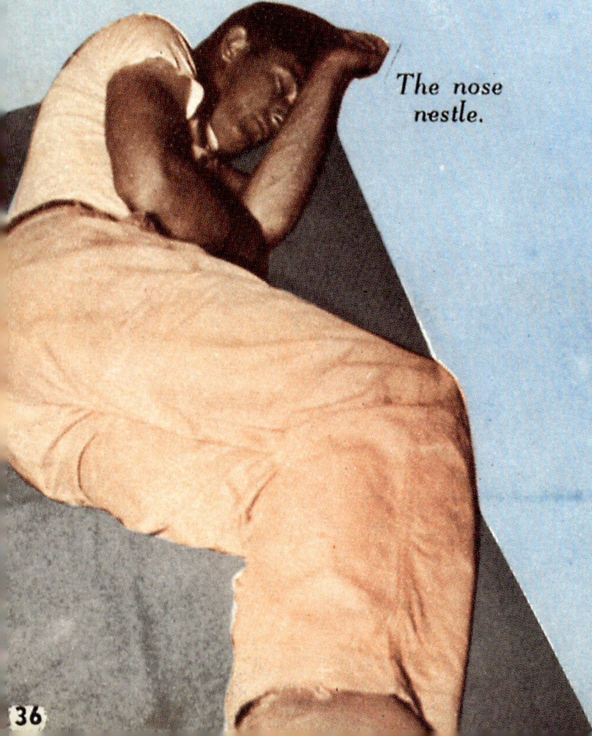

The nose nestle.

The one foot droop.

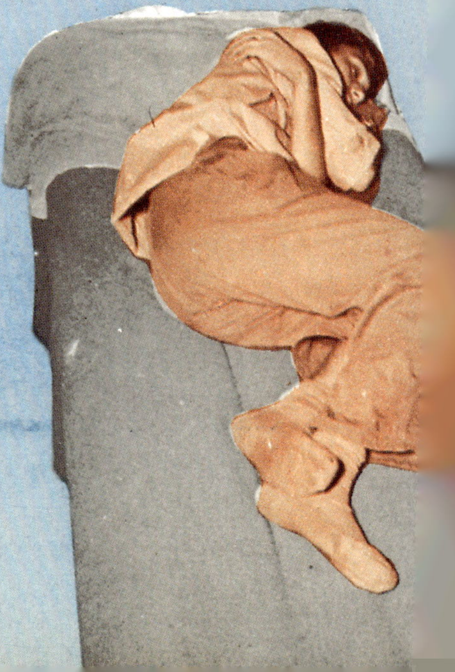

The self-embracing cuddle.

The CHAIRBORNE Division

No Purple Hearts
Awarded for
The callouses
You got at war
While sitting on
That tender spot
And working in
The Guinea hot.
But don't complain
And don't despair,
The war needs you
Right in that chair!

ON STRIKE

"Down with strikes!"
The papers roar,
"What a way
To win the war!"

If we may,
Correction, please—
Strikes here are
Necessities:

We're on strike
Against the foe—
Our picket line
Has Japs below!

QUIZ KIDS

Q. What's a Quiz Kid, Daddy?

A.: A very clever fellow, Snooks.

Q.: But why is he clever, Daddy?

A.: Because he's got brains.

Q.: What's brains?

A.: Brains is what licks the Japs, Snooks.

Q.: Do the Quiz Kids lick the Japs with their brains, Daddy?

A.: *That's* the 64-dollar question, Snooks!

OUR SUN-TANNED NEIGHBORS

Typical Papuan village on a Guinea beach. An idyllic scene—but you wouldn't care to linger.

ABOVE: A quintette of South Seas pin-up girls. Bewitching, ain't they? **RIGHT:** Missionary-trained natives call them "piccaninnies," just as we do. And like us, they sing lullabies to their children.

ABOVE: *Tribal dance drummer.*

ABOVE: Homes in the ocean. Some tribes prefer life on the blue. Natives are expert seamen—have effected sea rescues of pilots forced down over water.

ABOVE: Native belle, proudly displaying a new hair-do and . . . other things.

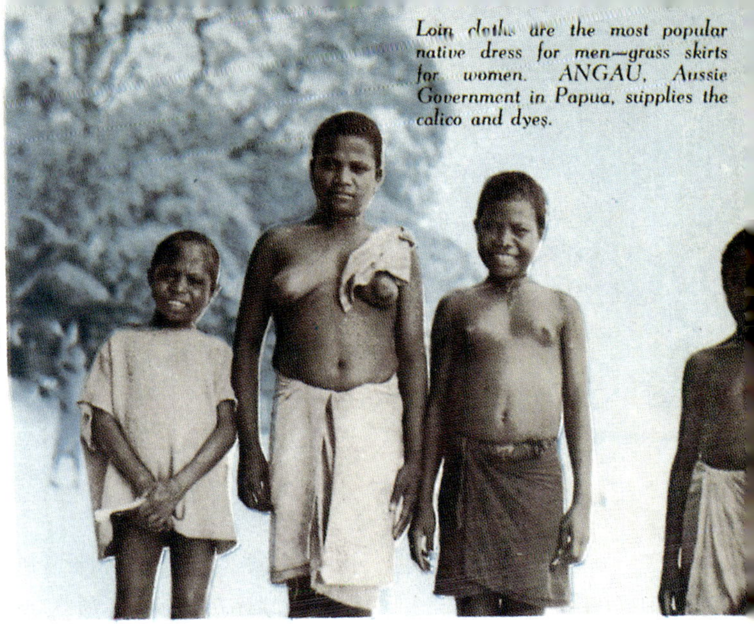

Loin cloths are the most popular native dress for men—grass skirts for women. ANGAU, Aussie Government in Papua, supplies the calico and dyes.

RIGHT: *The sago palm tree provides food, clothing and shelter for Papuans. Food: the heart of sago palm. Clothing: palm strips for grass dresses. Shelter: fronds for roofs and beds, lumber for huts and all construction.*

OVE: New Guinea vignette. Native soldier with rifle is ustralian-trained member of the Papuan Infantry. They fought the Japs and killed incredible numbers.

ABOVE: Native chief sports an Allied decoration and a GI fatigue hat (Lend-lease). **TOP CENTER:** Ten-minute break on a native WPA project. **TOP RIGHT:** Papuan police boy, most intelligent, best educated of all Guinea natives. **LOWER CENTER:** Papuans are master builders. They can measure by eye with astonishing accuracy. **LOWER RIGHT:** Native girl takes a sophisticated view of a candid camera fiend.

OUR FRIENDS THE *Buzz Job* BOMBERS

LEFT: A medium bomber flies mast-high over a Jap vessel, drops its eggs. **TOP LEFT:** Bull's eye! The ship lists, starts sinking. **BOTTOM LEFT:** Another addition to the Jap Navy's underwater fleet.

TOP CENTER: *The mediums go in at tree-top level, drop parachute frag bombs on enemy air field.* **TOP RIGHT:** *They don't kid around when they're chasing convoys. A medium once returned with a Jap ship's log blown into its engine.* **BOTTOM RIGHT:** *The Imperial Jap Air Force . . . somewhat less imperial.*

YOU GOTTA

KEEP 'EM *Flying!*

It's the boys in the basement who do the dirt

vork that gets the airbirds up through the ceiling. If they didn't meet their deadlines, vou wouldn't read the headlines!

THE guy with the monkey wrench will never be the hero of a bang-bang war film. Nor will his chest ever be weighed down with ribboned glory. But he's the baby who sends the bombers out—and brings them home. Airmen, who stake their lives on his skill and integrity, go up knowing he'll never let them down. No, you won't read much about the guy who keeps 'em flying—but there wouldn't be an Air Corps without him!

Then . . .

Keep . . .

'Em . . .

. . . Flying!

Jolly Rogers Throw a Party. And Man—

WHAT A NIGHT MISSION!

ABOVE: Post Office. First Special Delivery in many a moon for this lucky officer! **BOTTOM LEFT:** Newly-arrived shavetail gives a buzz job to a female hazer. **BOTTOM CENTER:** Heroes decorated for successful missions in the Sydney combat zone. **BOTTOM RIGHT:** Airman loses his wings at the jungle bar. **CIRCLES:** Boy meets girl—and a GI band plays "Jungle Bells" as the "snow" flies.

ABOVE: *Rug-cutters get in the gr*
and everybody else gets out of the

OVE: Nurses and Red Cross gals get blitzed with leaflet invitations he party, dropped from a B-24. **TOP CENTER:** 'Would-be gate-ers charge an MP Maginot Line. **TOP RIGHT:** The garden lounge are blind dates.

BENEATH: *Captain burns while MP's fiddle with his escort.* **LOWER RIGHT:** *Winner of JR's vote for the gal "I would like to fly with on an unescorted night mission."*

BELOW: Red Cross ga toasts her host.

BELOW: "I hate slacks!" mutters one of these JR's taking a down-under view of the dancing. **BOTTOM CENTER:** JR bomber team competes against a crew of nurses. Targets are glasses of—well, punch.

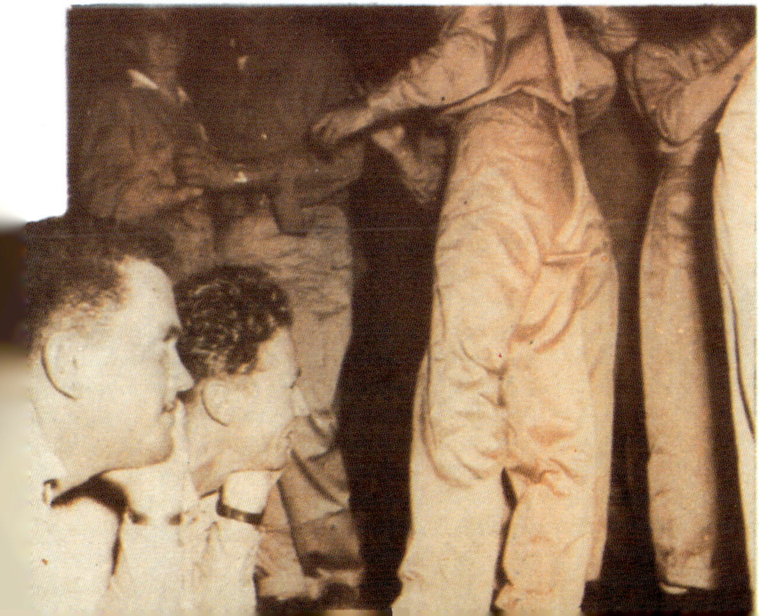

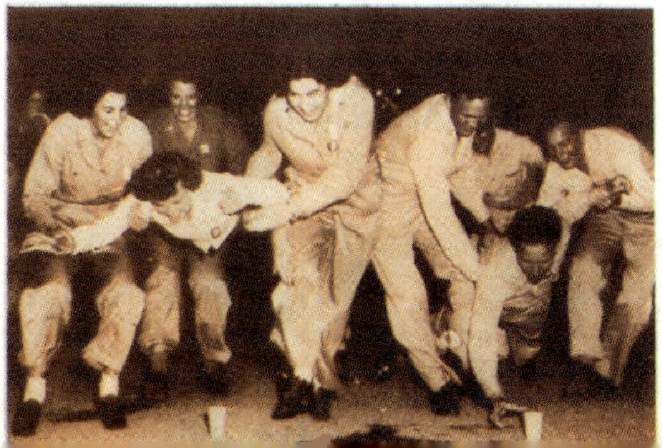

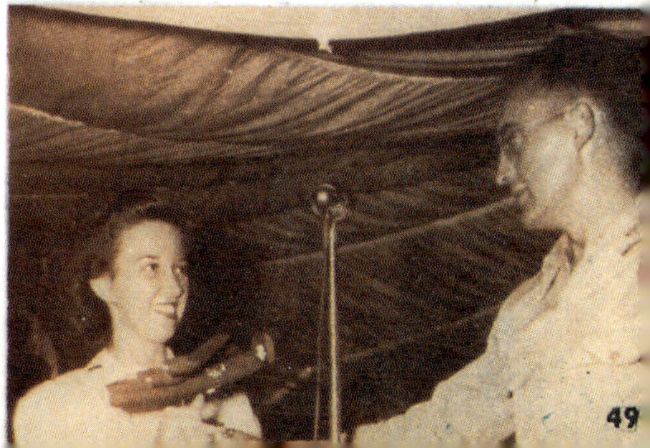

GUN GREMLINS

Bomber's ready, and we load her
Guns with ammo, as per quota.
That's our job; we do it well,
For we want to get the hell
Back to the land of Scotch and Soda!

BELOW: Helping to train gunners on the ground is one of the jobs of a "gun gremlin." These guardians of arms and ammunition can do everything with a .50 calibre but make it sing "Show Me the Way to Go Home."

BELOW: The "gun gremlins" operate a skeet range that helps explain the high record of Zero kills by JR gunners.

Hot Stuff HUSTLERS

OKAY, fellas, rise and shine,
  Tho' yonder stars are still agleam,
Ships are ready on the line
  Awaiting your part in the scheme.

No one likes the midnight chores,
  The sweat, the threat to every crew—
But better far to load on **yours**
  Than have **theirs** whistle down on you!

BULLETIN BOARD
KP ROSTER
DEPARTMENT MEMORANDUM
Dec 12 1944
NOW AVA
PX
purchas
Fur-lin
Mink Co
Guarante
Yachts
Airraid Wa
Marahuana Cigarettes
Zoot suits
ADDING MACHINE
—Courtesy of YANK Down Under
"Add one, Joe."
Courtesy of YANK Down Under
"He's the automatic pilot."
tsko Leyk
o Luciano
ano Mulke
MOSQUITOS DEMAND RIGHT TO LAND ON YANK DROMES
NETHERLANDS EAST INDIES
Miss Worthington,
her duty in view
join the WAC's.
Yank Spends Sydney Furlough at Concerts and Public Library!
SYDNEY, Aus.
any woman had ever received
GARBAG

SILENT PARTNERS

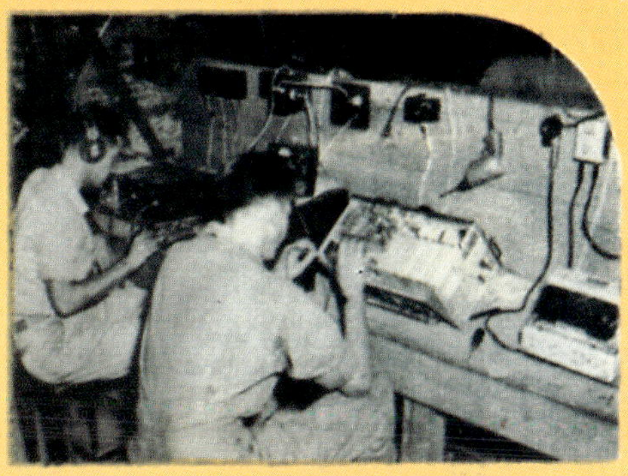

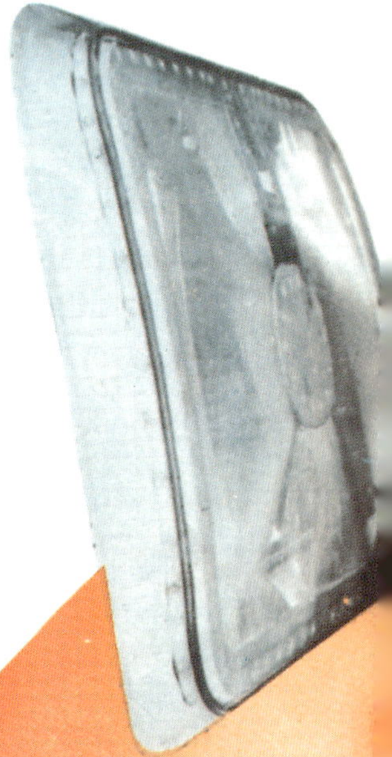

ABOVE: JOLLY ROGERS flying photographers, who bring back proof of what goes up when our bombs go down.

LEFT: *Taking photos of photos. Need for duplicate prints of photos keeps lab. men working at top speed far into the night.*

BELOW: Special drying machine speeds up the time necessary to make finished prints.

CIRCLE RIGHT: *Tropic weather plays hell with delicate camera equipment. Repair technicians have few idle moments.*

BELOW: Lab. men must know how to mix chemicals for hypo and developer.

LEFT: No job for fat-cats! The life of an aerial cameraman is rough—but rough. Try dressing like a deep-sea diver, and concentrating on getting pin-point, split-second photos from Olympian heights . . . while Zekes are making passes at your back-side, and flak is coming up like popcorn. Or wouldn't you rather?

CAMERA COMMANDOS

ABOVE: *Because photos of bombings are wanted pronto, time given to washing prints is cut down. Speed is paramount.*

BELOW: Notice the "dark room squint" on these JOLLY ROGERS. Rumor has it they come out into the sunlight only on pay-day.

BELOW: *Developing aerial film. First chance to see whether clouds obscured target hits.*

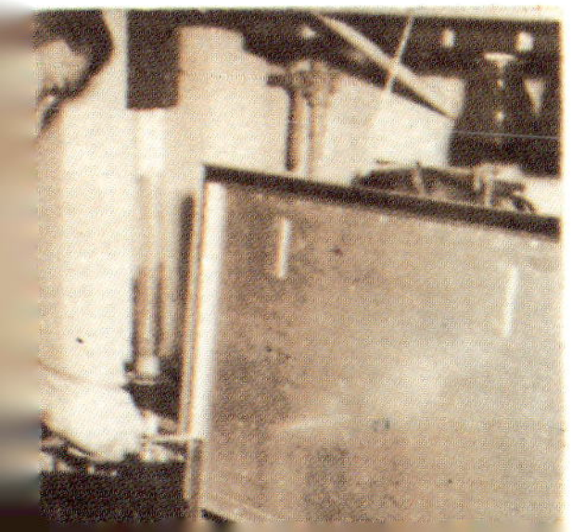

The CARRIER PIGEONS

YOU'VE never ever heard me gripe
At all the tripe on teletype,
Nor rage at air-to-ground—oh, no!
Nor do I growl at Morse that's foul
Or switchboards that have lost a bowel—
I lost my voice three years ago!

I can't imagine why the hell
Alexander Graham Bell
Was never swiftly boiled in oil.
The same for Mister Marconi—
Since all they've ever done for me
Is break my %&?£%!& back with toil!

HURRY
RUSH

FAST
AT ONCE
QUICKLY

EMERGENCY
IMMEDIATE
SOS

Rogues Gallery

ABOVE: When the JR's give the Japs a death-kiss, these boys tell. Furnishing facts, figures and fancy phrases, they've spread the fame of the "best damn heavy, etc.," throughout the world.

BELOW: Sailors with an Air Corps outfit? Sure! These boys run the JOLLY ROGERS crash-boat in shark-infested Guinea waters.

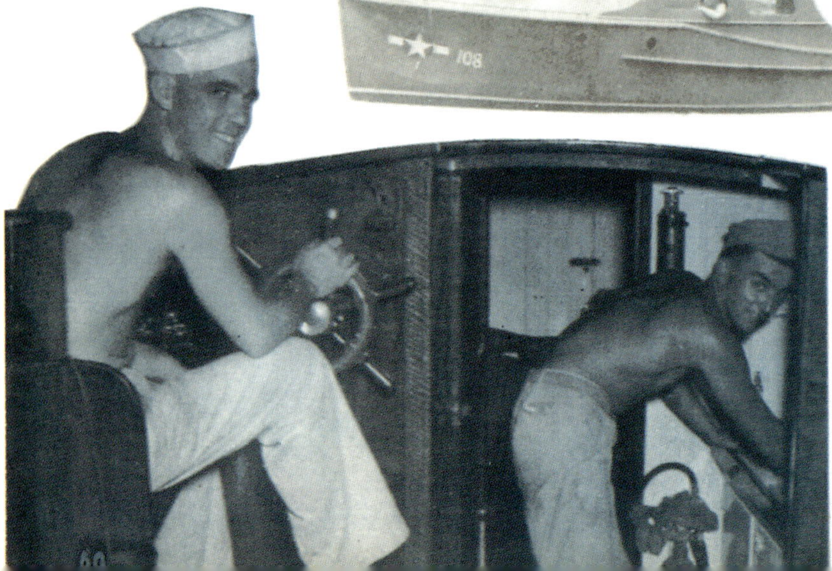

LEFT: *Japs no like flying office Lieut.-Colonel Scott and Maj Hart. Both are contenders f world's record of longest comb hours. Last tally (some tim ago) showed flier Scott a proaching 600 mark, whi runner-up Hart had turned th 500 corner. • What was that yo said about combat fatigue?*

ABOVE: Three trouble - shooti Musketeers. These plane doct can cure a bomber of everythi but halitosis.

LEFT: Zebra Convention. Three - dozen (count 'em) stripes represented in this bevy of top-kicks. G'wan, they do not eat babies, either!

STRIP *Gear* ARTISTS

OH, say, can you see
By the dawn's early light
The trucks gloomily
Rolling airbirds to flight?

Then home, James, to work,
And the day really starts,
Fixing jeeps for some jerk
Whose head needs spare parts!

ABOVE: Outside of twenty enemy bombers, nothing but fresh eggs can induce a Guinea GI to rise at the bitter dawn hour. But in spite of sweating out the long chow line, looks as though our boy here missed the boat again. Oh, well, have a wienie—and the crying towel will be right up.

RIGHT: *Here we see our hero sweating out the PX line. Since he may have a birthday or a baby before he gets to the counter, he wisely brings along his cot and a copy of "GONE WITH THE WIND."*

BELOW: *The mail, transported* via *Pony Express because of the shortage of bicycles, finally arrives after sweating it out a century or two. The mail clerk takes a few days to separate his personal mail from the unimportant residue. Then Mail Call begins. But somehow, though your tent-mate Joe Blotz rates 47 letters, all you get is a postcard advertising straw hats. So you sweat it out until the bottom V-mail, which is never yours anyhow. Then you go back to your tent and sweat out next month's Mail Call.*

Sweating It Out

WITH THE JOLLY ROGERS

"HOW'S it goin', Sad Sack?"

"Sweatin' it out, boy, sweatin' it out."

In those three words you have life on this violent-tempered island for the JOLLY ROGERS. Whatever the matter of the moment, they're all sweating it out, figuratively and literally. What used to be a simple matter of putting a nickel in the slot now requires the patience of Gandhi and trust in the Lord.

In addition to the tall and fancy types of sweating out illustrated here, most of the dogfaces (many of whom haven't been home for three years) are still sweating out their first WAC, WAVE, Republican Governor, States furlough, Stage Door Canteen, zoot suit, and Frank Sinatra. It's a great life—if your sweat glands don't weaken!

"Everybody gets a furlough but me!" Cheer up, bud—you can go when they come back. (If you live that long!)

LEFT: Having eaten, you may be called upon to heed the necessities of nature. Unfortunately, as a rule, so are the rest of the squadron. So you line up again and sweat it out, tossing occasional dark glances at occupants inconsiderate enough to regard the edifice as a Public Library.

RIGHT: *For sheer agony nothing beats sweating out a promotion. For years, you've been sweating and bucking (civilian translation: apple polishing) to impress upon the C.O. what a bright boy you are. But it's always the same story—no vacancy on the T.O. Which is just T.S., if you know what we mean.*

BELOW: *The miracle happens and your furlough orders are cut. The only hitch—sweating out a* DC-3 *to Aussie. After two years of weary thumb-wagging, you might get discouraged and come back. But if you finally get passage on what is sarcastically referred to as a boat, you start sweating out submarines. If you go by plane, you sweat out that cough in the No. 1 engine. But you always sleep soundly en route . . . curled up on the nice soft beard you've got by the time you get down.*

ABOVE: Have you ever tried living out of one pair of pants, two pairs of socks, one undershirt, and two pairs of trunks—one of which has a **damned** inconvenient hole? That's what sweating out a clothing issue means. Your only hope of melting the Supply Sergeant's heart is with a diamond-tip drill. "But look at that hole!" squeals our Sad Sack. Snarls the unfeeling villain: "Well, hop around on the other foot!"

BELOW: *You do some tall and fancy sweating when you hear about the number of bombers the Japs just flew in up north. Then you start sweating out your share of foxhole time on those beautiful moonlit tropic nights. But when you're on detail, brother, you just sweat. Altogether, you sure need an* AWFUL *lot of salt tablets in this man's Army!*

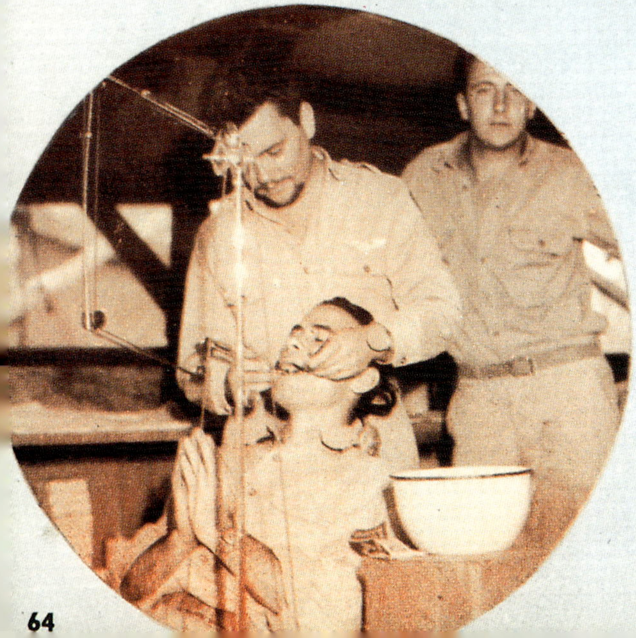

ASPIRIN ASSASSINS

The GI is a funny guy,
He damns "pillrollers" to the sky
    In manner energetic.
That's when everything is jake --
But when he gets a bellyache . . .
    He screams out for a "medic"

Misfit MAESTROS

WHATEVER you want, there ain't
any here,
So pardon me, bud, while I shed a tear.
I know you've been waiting half a year
To draw all that most essential gear,
But your day will come, so never fear.
In the meantime, bud—don't bend my ear!

NEITHER RAIN NOR HAIL NOR SLEET NOR SNOW . . .

Heroes when the mail's in—villains when it's not. That's the sad fate of an Army postman.

NO SHIRTEE . . . NO TICKEE . . .

Volunteers for the Army's dirtiest job—laundry. Blessings on you, little men . . . may all your troubles be Rinso bubbles.

DIAMOND BRACELETS WOOLWORTH DOESN'T SELL, BABY . . .

"Okay, who's next? . . . No, we ain't got any Cashmere Bookay toilet soap . . . Ya kin only have one candy bar . . . Aincha got any smaller change?"

SEE THE CHAPLAIN *for your*

T.S. TICKET

Good For One Crying Towel

With your share of GI woe
To the Chaplain you must go.
Can it help you? Oh, dear no—
But you'll feel better, even so!

"No, dammit, this ain't goin' to Sydney!"

"They came over with the original Squadron == a couple of brothers named Wright, from Dayton, Ohio.."

Courtesy of YANK Down Under

. . . and our own OSCARS of the WALDORF

YANK DOWN UNDER *featured this event on its cover. The picket sign tells the story. The gentleman with the raised cleaver is, understandably, the long-suffering Mess Sergeant. But d'ye think this one-man strike stopped the* JOLLY ROGERS *from crossing the picket line? Hell, no—they just* **love** *their bully beef!*

If succulent scenes like this are hard to recognize or believe, jog your memory back to last Thanksgiving. Yep, one day a year we live to eat, and 364 days a year . . .

In God We Trust

We didn't have to be coaxed to church. Not flying as often as we did!

"YEA, though I walk through the valley of the shadow of death, I will fear no evil; for thou art with me."

Whether Protestant, Catholic or Jewish, every soldier in Guinea could attend his own services, observe his own religious holidays.

CAMP

RIGHT: This fine example of a jungle-happy Jolly Roger, making like Mr. Esky at a juicy Vargas pin-up, appeared in ESQUIRE. Look at those eyes pop — no wonder ESQUIRE was banned!

RIGHT: *Here it is—the dinkum oil! Real jungle juice, the champagne of New Guinea. One drink of this stuff and your toes fall off, your spine rattles and your ears chase each other around your face. What's left melts.*

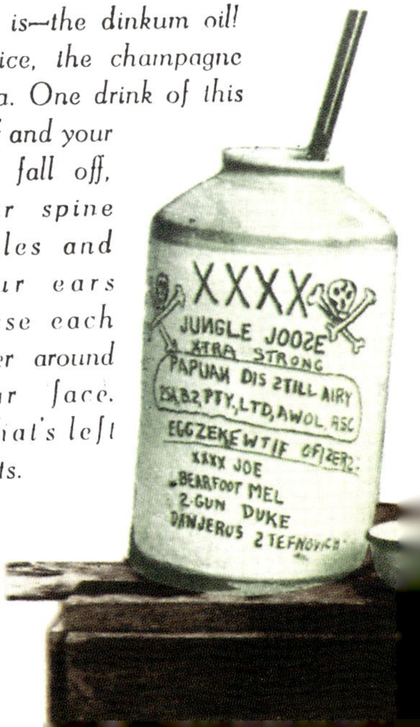

VIGNETTES

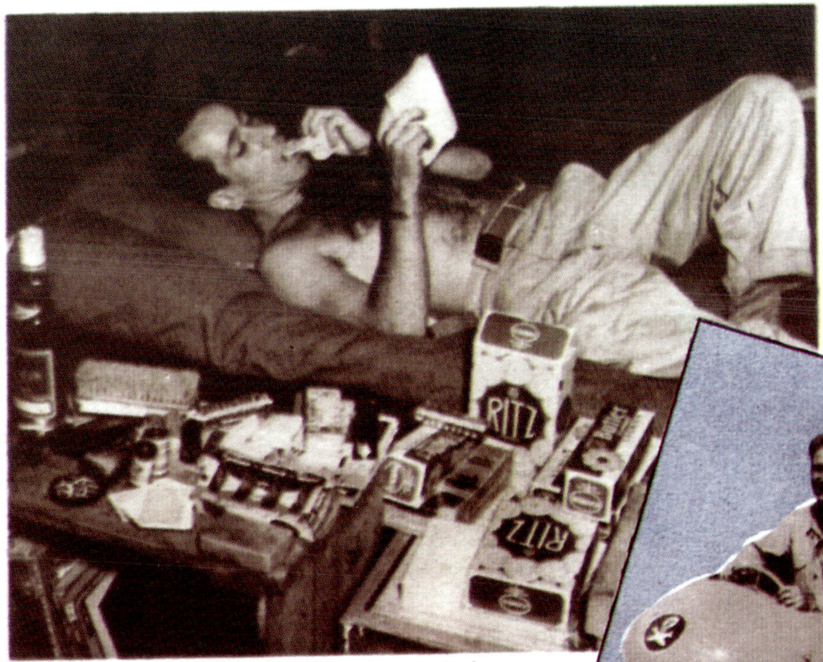

ABOVE: Oh, hardships, hardships all the way. Here's a Jolly Roger performing his morning spine-bashing exercises. Notice the well-stocked pantry. The selfish lug—why'nt he send some comforts to the poor starving civilians in the States?

Guinea jam session, Harlem style. Here's the first authentic photo of a Fuzzy Wuzzy hepcat. Man, is he out of this world!

ABOVE: This whacky super-car actually works! Made by a Jolly Roger out of spare airplane parts, it can do 20 m.p.h. But not more, as its inventor is hopelessly explaining to an airstrip M.P. Picture made a YANK DOWN UNDER cover.

ABOVE: A Jolly Roger's pet reacts, even as you and I, to a choice bit of plane gallery art. Wouldn't you stand up on your hind legs and go woof woof, too?

ABOVE: Much-heard lament: "Dammit, newspapers, newspapers and newspapers—all a year old! No wonder there's no room for real mail!"

MISSION SUCCESSFUL

A new crew fresh from the States goes on its first mission with the JR's. And it's a hot one!

1. "So these are the JOLLY ROGERS!" The arrivals size up the unit they've heard so much about.

2. Eager beavers all, they climb into the camp truck on the double. Their first Guinea scenery.

3. First JOLLY ROGERS chow. What, Montmorenc —no oyster cocktails? Not even fingerbowls?

8. Baptism at last! The new crew is assigned to its first mission. Briefing begins . . .

9. . . . and Col. Rogers breaks the news. The first mass daylight raid on fortress Rabaul!

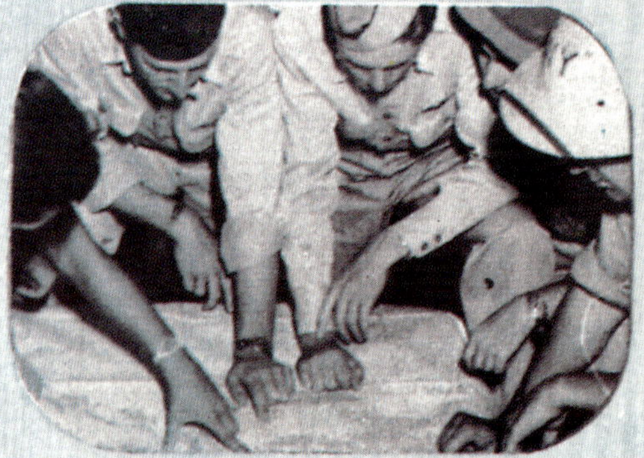

10. Navigator points out crew's target on map. Weather forecast: plenty hot, fellas!

11. New crew studies photos of target area. A body who's calm is a liar or he ain't goin'!

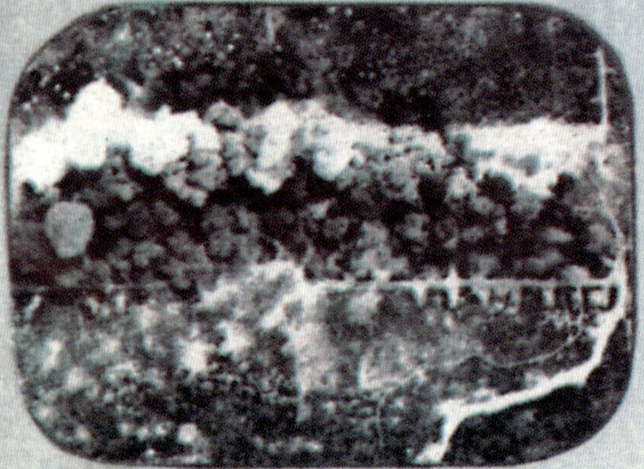

16. Bingo! Bull's-eye for bombardier and T.S. for Tokyo! They turn for home, but the Nips . . .

17. Press home a 50-plane attack! Guns get red-hot firing. Here's one Nip headed for the drink.

18. Anxious ground crews sweat the boys home from the long mission. Eager eyes scan the skies . . .

19. And here they come! Worried groundmen cou them. Our crew slides in for a smooth landing.

Sleeping gear is drawn from Supply. Tonight ill be their first time under mosquito bars.

5. Shooting the breeze with JR old-timers. So many questions, the bull session runs overtime.

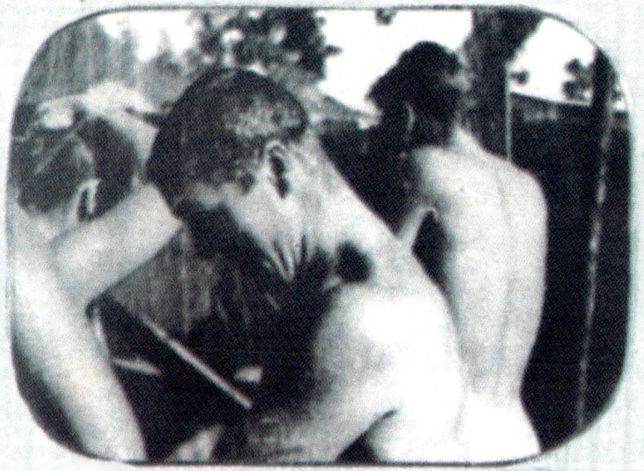

6. Next day. A nice cold shower in the morning to start the day off wrong. They'll learn.

7 Intensive training begins. Gunners to skeet range, bombardier into this weird contraption.

2. Sweating out take-off. To go or not to go—that the question. Time dawdles on!

13. At last the line-up—and what a breeze! Don't push, buddy . . . your turn's coming!

14. And here we go for the take-off. Then tense hours over enemy seas. Finally the target, and . . .

15. Bombs away! Gunners man their .50's tautly, as clouds of enemy fighters swarm to attack.

Red Cross girls make it "so nice to come home." Man, does that ground feel delicious!

21. Here's how! No longer a "dodo," a new "vet" toasts his luck on a hot but handsome mission.

22. Gunners renew their life insurance. These babies are sweet to shoot—but hell to clean!

23. Chalk up three Zekes. The baptism of fire is over—and another proud new crew is "in."

These Were Our Brothers

A PLEDGE

GREAT speeches will be made and memorials erected for our comrades who did not return. But no words, no stone, can tell the grief engraved in the hearts of those who did return. The fliers who died in enemy skies were our friends. We ate, slept and fought beside them. These were our brothers.

No, we shall not forget them. Because we cannot. Their laughter, their voices still ring in our memory with shocking reality. The final cup of Victory, however sweet, will be bitter because they will not be there to share it with us.

Avenge them? Yes, our guns have avenged them against the enemy in the air, our bombs have erected flaming memorials to them on the ground. This is as they would have wished.

But it will not restore them to us. We can only take consolation in the eternal reward which must now be theirs, as surely as there is an Ultimate Justice. We can only wish them Godspeed, and assure them that our love for them has not died because they are no longer with us.

But more, we vow—***and this time we shall keep the vow***—that these honored dead shall not have died in vain. We will not rest until the tyranny of Axis dictators is stamped off the face of the earth. And we will fight with the same passionate fury for a peace that shall be everlasting, and a world where all men may enjoy life, liberty and the pursuit of happiness.

This is how we shall remember the dead. We can do no less. For these men were our brothers.

Presenting
The JOLLY ROGERS
COMBAT CREWS

AS this section of the JOLLY ROGERS book goes to press, word comes that the crews whose pictures you are about to see on the next pages have led the first mass daylight raids against the Jap-held Philippines, and received credit for "all bombs on target."

COE
Steele
Clyde
Miles

Answer to a GI's prayer. Movie star trips the light fantastic with a GI, who is no advertisement for Burma Shave.

LEFT: This bird also plays the zither with his feet, but he couldn't bring it with him.

RIGHT: Film stars Gary Cooper, Phyllis Brooks and Una Merkel autograph some JR first editions for Tokyo. Lucky Japs!

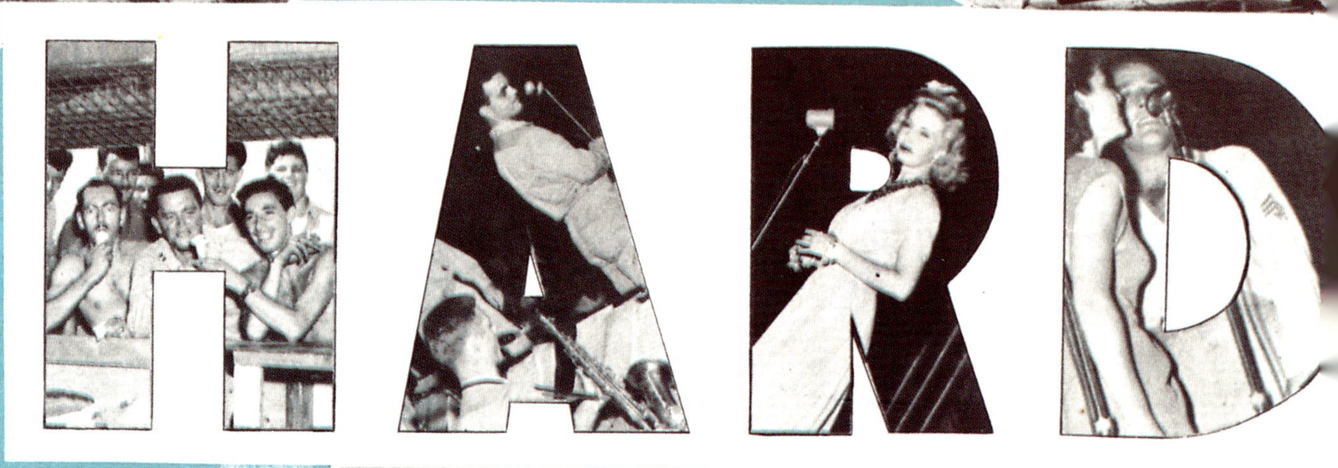

LEFT: GI female impersonator grinds out some New Guinea bumps in a strip hula. Who's jungle happy?

RIGHT: Funnyman Jack Benny inspects a JR ship named after him. The girl? Well, it ain't Mrs. Roosevelt!

Radio singer Jean Durrell dishes out ice cream cones at the PX. What a war, what a war!

IT'S a crazy war when amous stars of stage and screen can pop out of nowhere to give you a show right in the jungle. And in the flesh. But man, didn't we appreciate them! Our heartfelt thanks to these swell entertainers who made us forget the war, and where we were, for a brief, happy while. Hardships like these we could suffer all the time!

RIGHT: Joe E. Brown makes with the mouth in a bit of clowning at a JR show.

ABOVE: Carol Landis joins the JOLLY ROGERS. Isn't this a dainty dish to set before a thousand dogfaces?

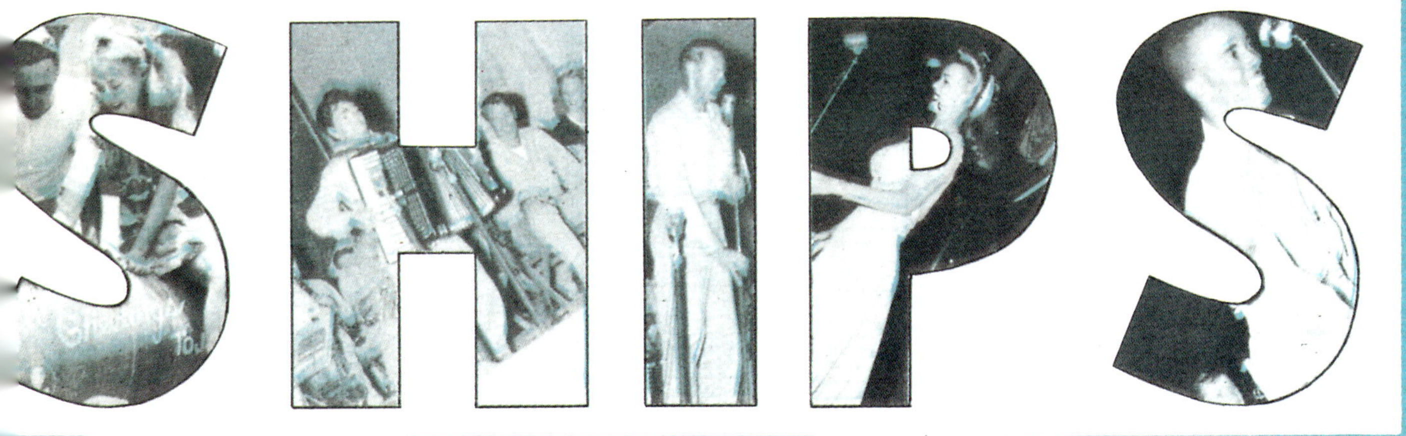

BELOW: These hep cats used to drive the neighbors batty. Now we listen and cheer. What a helluva difference a few thousand miles make!

GI Jive for GI Joes. Doesn't have to be good—as long as it's good and loud. New Guinea Gallup Poll showed Fuzzy Wuzzies thought it was the nuts.

Ekstrand

Harter

Briggs

Robeck

Ekstrand	
D.S.C.	1
Silver Star	58
D.F.C.	250
Soldier's Medal	7
Purple Heart	35
Air Medal	980
Total	1,331

Harter	
Silver Star	32
D.F.C.	166
Soldier's Medal	11
Purple Heart	21
Bronze Star Medal	2
Air Medal	841
Total	1,073

Briggs	
R.A.A.F. D.F.C.	1
Legion of Merit	1
Silver Star	18
D.F.C.	231
Soldier's Medal	7
Purple Heart	69
Air Medal	790
Bronze Star Medal	2
Total	1,119

Robeck	
Silver Star	78
D.F.C.	199
Soldier's Medal	7
Purple Heart	25
Air Medal	736
Bronze Star Medal	3
Total	1,050

THE BIG FOUR Who Led Their Men to Glory

3349

AIR MEDALS

150

PURPLE HEARTS

32

SOLDIER'S MEDALS

186

SILVER STARS

846

DISTINGUISHED FLYING CROSSES

4,573 Decorations

Won by Jolly Rogers in First Twenty-Eight Months of Combat*

*These awards are as official figures from September, 1942 to December, 1944.

Unit Breakdown of Awards on Page Opposite

Also Awarded—

1 Distinguished Service Cross

1 R.A.A.F. Distinguished Flying Cross

1 Legion of Merit

7 Bronze Star Medals

CHEST HARDWARE —Worn Over Valiant Hearts

NURSERY RHYMES for TOKYO

Illustrated with photos of Jolly Rogers in action

Little Bo Jap

The Japanese race has lost its face
And don't know where to find it.
The intelligence man has a marvellous plan
To not only find—but to grind it!

Georgie Porgie

Georgie Porgie, aerial photo,
Clicks the harbors while on recco,
When the prints come out okay—
Next thing clicked is "Bombs Away!"

Jack and Jill

Jack and Jill flew over the hill
And far out over the water,
For just to drown the Japs sailed down
Right where they hadn't oughta!

Little Jack Horner

Little Jack Horner rolls round the corner
With eggs for the Japanese Diet.
Japs, who like rice, yell, "Eggs not nice!"
But once they taste 'em—they're quiet!

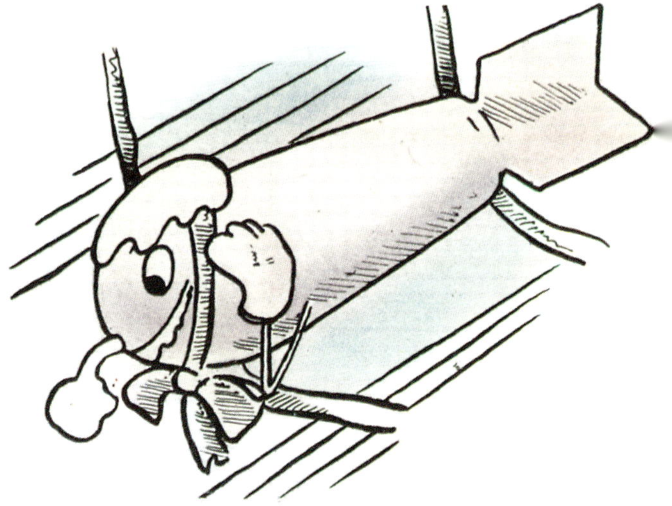

Rockaby Bomb-Bay

Rockaby baby, in your bomb-bay,
When the doors open, this is your day,
Down you will go, scream as you fall,
Up will come pieces of Japanese gall!

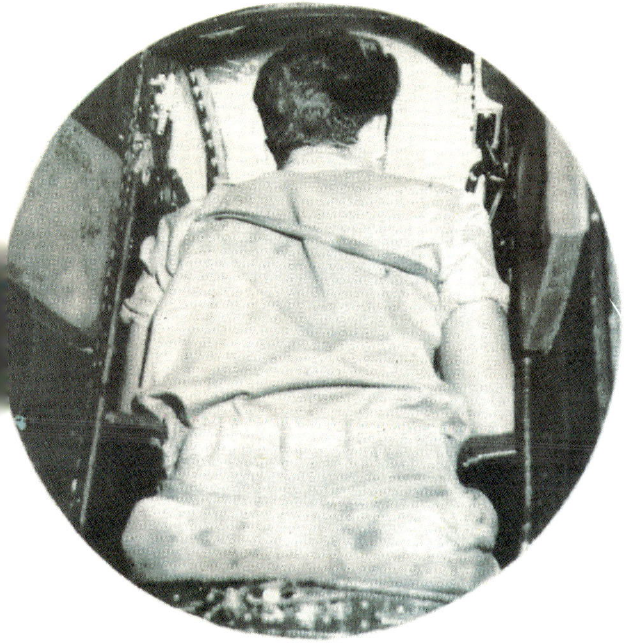

Hickory Dickory Dock

Hickory dickory dock,
The Zekes fly round the clock,
  Tail-gunner shot one
  With his little wee gun,
Just to put in his Christmas sock!

Engineer Muffet

Engineer Muffet sat in his turret
* Eating his heart out all day,*
Along came Nip flights and sat in his sights—
* Now Muffet is cheerful and gay!*

Hi Diddle Diddle

Hi diddle diddle, Zekes shouldn't fiddle
  With waist gunners ready to meet 'em,
The little dogs laughed, which proved they were daft—
  Ancestors now pleased to greet 'em!

Nursery rhymes have always been favored for teaching infants too young to attend school. Out of respect for the infantile minds of our enemies, who apparently are still not able to read our hand-writing on the wall, we offer these nursery rhymes for Tokyo. With humble apologies to Mother Goose.

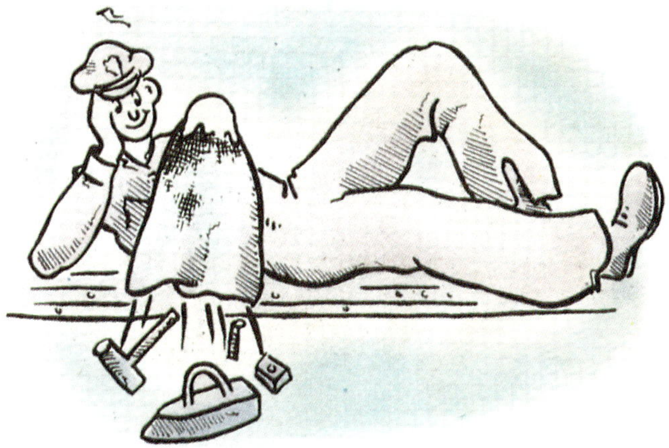

Twinkle, Twinkle, Little Star

Twinkle, twinkle, little star,
Navigator wonders where we are,
Up above the sky so blue,
If he is lost, boy—so are you!

Humpety Dumped

Humpety dumped a shipment of steel,
Humpety dumped it with a great zeal,
All the Nip coolies and all the Nip men
Couldn't put Hollandia together again!

Jolly Rogers ALL-AMERICAN Bomber Teams

Outstanding Crews Who Helped Make Southwest Pacific History.

S. JOHNSON

CURRIE

OLSEN

WHITLOCK

Here's How You Recognise 'Em

Command Pilot

Pilot

Bombardier

Navigator

Air Crew Member

Aerial Gunner

TAYLOR

RAINARD

KLINE

EKSTRAND

TEAMWORK

Throw that pass! Block that kick!
Take the ball! Fall back quick!
Watch those Zekes at two o'clock!
Got my eye right on 'em, Doc.

Take a lead! Watch that fly!
Now go home! Score is tie!
Hurry up, please—Danny's hit!
Take my gun—I'll bandage it.

Ring that goal! Pass it back!
Block that man! Shoot it, Mac!
Hit the silk, boys—gas is low!
Hell, let's see how far she'll go!

ADAMS

HOLMES

JOHNSON

ROBECK

DALEY

ARANT

SANXTER

SMITH

RAIG

MENGE

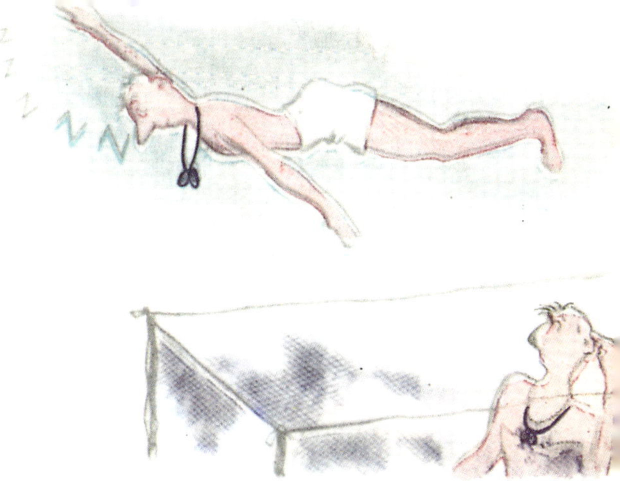

HOWALTER

VOWELL

COOLIDGE

ARTIN

SYLVERNALE

PORTER

HALLADAY

KUBISKIE

SAVAGE

ROGERS

Here's How You Recognise an All-American.

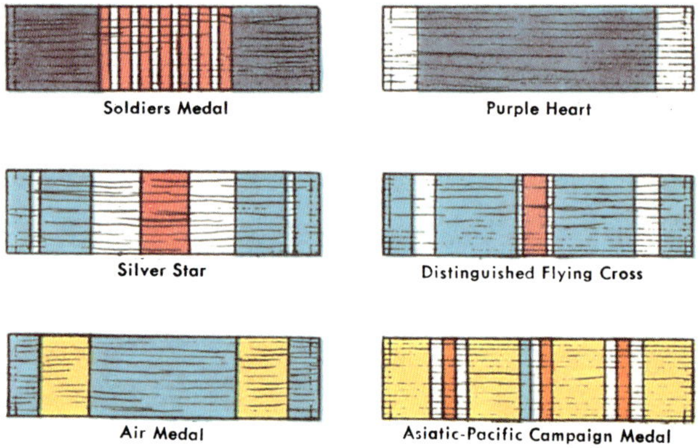

ELLIOTT

KOSTER

SHAFFER

RILEY

"AIRCRAFT AGE" MAGAZINE

Selects First

ALL-AMERICAN BOMBER TEAM

—and all Jolly Rogers!

The American flying magazine, "AIRCRAFT AGE," in a recent issue published an article called "All-American Bomber Team" by M/Sgt. Jules Archer. In this article the world's first such combat team is nominated . . . each position in the All-American bomber filled by an outstanding Jolly Rogers flier. Among those nominated were Lt. Olsen, All-American Pilot, and S/Sgt. William Simon, All-American Right Waist Gunner, both of whom were lost together in action.

PRIMER FOR DODOS

This page is intended for the instruction of new crews, particularly on their first combat missions to Sydney. On these hazardous flights, even the most experienced JOLLY ROGER bachelor may be overcome by combat fatigue or run into unexpected ambushes. Because we realize that even such dangers will not deter JOLLY ROGERS from volunteering for this perilous mission, we have prepared an abbreviated guide to the jungles of Sydney. To be prepared for all emergencies, observe the following precautions:—

LESSON ONE

This is an anti-aircraft position. There's no love here for Yank fliers! Clear out of the area.

LESSON TWO

This is a balloon barrage, meant to snare you. Don't approach this target unless you're willing to pay the price.

LESSON THREE

This is a slippery runway. If you don't lower your flaps you're liable to make a crash landing.

Sydney, Australia.

LESSON FOUR

This is a booby trap. Be careful, or it'll cost you an arm and a leg.

LESSON FIVE

This is a friendly job. Look for identification markings. If she wiggles her wings, you can make a few friendly passes.

LESSON SIX

This is interception. You can't expect a milk run every time. But don't let it swerve you off course.

LESSON SEVEN

This is the drink, in which many good fliers have been drowned. Dangerous when you're already flying a tight f

LESSON EIGHT

These are extra pounds, which won't weigh you down on the return trip. But don't salvo more than you have to!

Eager Beaver, made famous by Major Whitlock, was celebrated in an article called PORTRAIT OF A LIBERATOR *in* PLANE TALK *Magazine, July, 1944.*

EAGER BEAVER. She had almost a hundred missions before she returned to the States to sell war bonds. Lead ship on the first daylight mission on Rabaul, she had been in many hot scraps in her career. Three Zeros and three Jap ships were chalked up on her venerable sides when she retired.

SILVER STAR BOMBERS

YANKEE DOODLE **DANDY** had a charmed life for 100 missions. Although the enemy had attacked her persistently, she had shaken them off like bothersome fleas, destroying seven Zekes in her year of life. On her 101st mission she straggled from the formation over Hollandia, and three Zekes shot her down. Her demise was genuinely mourned as only an old and faithful friend can be mourned.

HELLZAPOPPIN *the first mission of the Jolly Rogers, the first daylight strike against Rabaul, the first against Ambon, the first long range strike against Kendari, and was the first to retire from combat to the States, with 950 combat hours to her credit, more than any other plane in the SWPA had at that time. She collected the scalps of seven Zekes and one ship, under the tutelage of Buzzin' Johnny Johnson, celebrated in the* SATURDAY EVENING POST.

EIGHT BALL didn't belie her ominous name. She had one Zeke and one cargo ship chalked up when she folded her nose wheel. Alexishafen Ack-Ack practically tore off her wing, but didn't down her. On lone recco near Wewak, twelve Zekes hopped her. Lt. Shafer took her to water level, where the crew fought out the uneven battle. Score: six Zekes shot down, three probables! And holes galore for EIGHT BALL. Her record at retirement: 11 Zekes, 5 probables, 2 ships. Japs certainly were behind the EIGHT BALL!

Any combat man will tell you that his bomber is more than a robot. When airmen speak of their B-24's, it's with personal pride and affection. This page and the two that follow present some of the most famous Jolly Rogers Liberators.

MOBY DICK, shown here with her offspring, a Piper Cub called Moby Dick, Jr., was so famous that her whole unit was named after her. Four Jap planes and three Jap ships fell to her. On a night mission over Rabaul she went into a dive, and pulled out at 470 miles per hour! After bombing the Lae convoy, MOBY DICK returned home with over 200 holes in her body. She was always in the thick of the roughest strikes, smacked her bombs right on the target, and only too often came home looking like a soup-strainer.

COOKIE had a hell of a time over Rabaul on a night mission. Caught in powerful searchlights, the Ack-Ack almost smothered her. Lt. Cook took a desperate chance and put her in a 400 m.p.h. dive, escaping successfully. Next morning's checkup showed she needed a new pair of wings! Another close call came when she had to fly at water level through a storm—"so low we could have taken a bath, if we had soap." But she made base safely after over 9 hours of instrument flying. Her scoreboard: seven Zekes.

GONE WITH THE WIND celebrated her 100th combat mission by participating in the first daylight raid on Hollandia, with all bombs on the target, tagging some planes on the ground for good measure. In on all the "firsts," including the first daylights on Wewak and Rabaul, she rolled up a tally of five Zekes shot down, and several probables. In May she was holding the SWPA record for heavy bomber combat time.

THE DUDE brought joy to the hearts of its hard-worked ground crew. She went for over 400 hours without a generator change, and never had an engine change. This sturdy baby flew through some 60 rough missions (by May), knocked down two Jap planes, and sank two Jap ships.

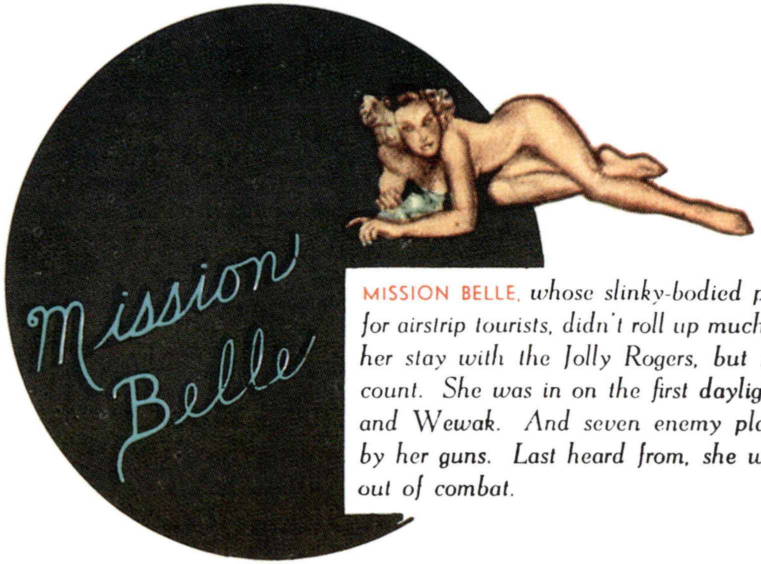

MISSION BELLE, whose slinky-bodied pin-up was a magnet for airstrip tourists, didn't roll up much combat time during her stay with the Jolly Rogers, but she made that time count. She was in on the first daylight kills over Rabaul and Wewak. And seven enemy planes were destroyed by her guns. Last heard from, she was still around—but out of combat.

TOKIO EXPRESS was a real pin-up plane. Lt. General Kenney asked for her picture to hang up in his trophy room. During her 48 missions before return to the States, she quietly sent nine Zekes where they belonged, and dunked a 6,000 ton merchant vessel.

PUDGY threw her weight around Jap skies with good results—knocking out three Zeros and retiring two of his Imperial Majesty's imperial navy. Also on the first daylight over fortress (now ex-fortress) Rabaul, she ran up her number of missions to over ninety, when last counted.

CONNELL'S SPECIAL *was the only "Silver Job" with the Jolly Rogers during her stay. She was the first of the modified B-24's to make their debut in the* SWPA. *The choice of Colonel Rogers for his own "joy" rides over the enemy,* CONNELL'S SPECIAL *led the Jolly Rogers on many missions. Strictly a tub-dunker, she sank four Jap ships, and damaged another, scrapping 7,500 tons of enemy steel.*

STAR DUSTER joined the Jolly Rogers when she had the distinction of being the only B-24 with a belly gun. That rather surprised the first Nips who attacked her from below. The first was blown to hell—the others beat it to hell away. STAR DUSTER proudly carried a General on her first night mission over Rabaul. On one of her missions her rudder cable was shot away, but she murdered the Zeke that did it, and another for good measure. Boat-hungry, STAR DUSTER beached one, and also skip-bombed a four-ship convoy. Badly hit, she had to salvo everything she could and make a safe landing at a nearby base. Before returning to the States with 67 missions, she'd sunk two boats, damaged one, and shot down no less than eleven Zeros. Only one of her crew was ever wounded.

GOLDEN LADY was named after the luscious female painted on both her sides. Her first wound was a 20 mm. shell through her side on a long recco, for which the attacking Zero was shot down. During the first daylight over Rabaul, her crew bagged five more. Often flying two missions a day, she needed a real going over after 500 hours, which included installation of four new power plants. Facelifted, she went back into action . . . collecting her share of Ack-Ack, one fragment of which nicked a navigator in the leg and made a rummage sale of flying clothes around the flight deck. Last heard from she was a grand old dame with 800 hours, 97 missions and 6 Zeros to her credit.

REMEMBER

. . . When an Infantry private *(above)* visited our Nadzab camp right after the invasion of Hollandia, showing his captured Jap trophies to Colonels Brandt and MacDonald? And had to lend them to some 100 Jolly Rogers, each of whom shamelessly posed with the trophies?

When Major Layhee and his fiancee nurse (below) decided to tie the knot right in New Guinea? And their honeymoon was spent in a General's villa at Port Moresby?

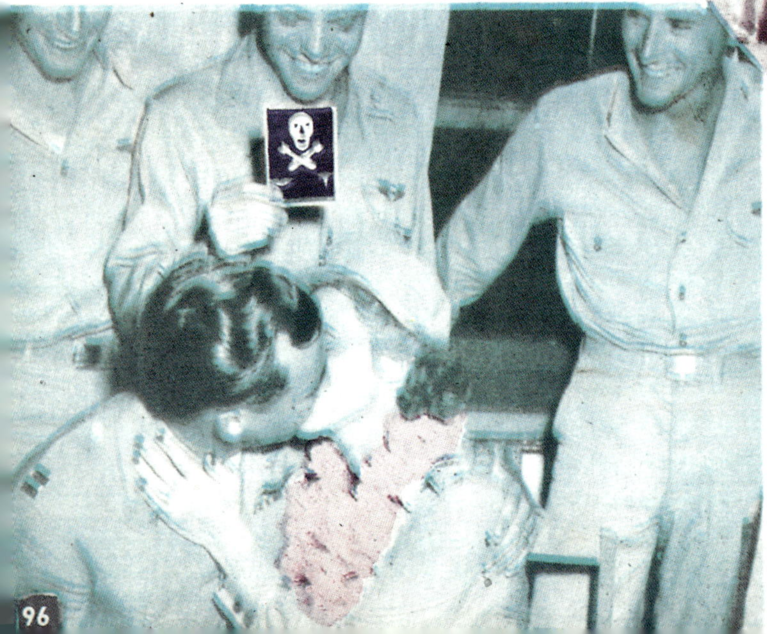

RIGHT: When the Jolly Rogers were so damn rushed during their stay at Port Moresby that three Liberators had to be serviced in one revetment?

ABOVE: When the Jolly Rogers raised their flag for the first time, at Nadzab, after their outstanding victory at Hollandia? And when Ken's Men swiped it? (Someone said they last saw it over a Sydney bar!)

RIGHT: *When "Hell's Angels" met with this sad fate?*

When these cute tricks from the USA came out to show us a few things we'd been missing, lo, these many years?

ABOVE: *When Colonel Rogers finally said goodbye to the outfit to which he had lent his name, and turned it over to Colonel Bullis to continue in the traditions we had made a byword in the Southwest Pacific?*

WHEN . . . ?

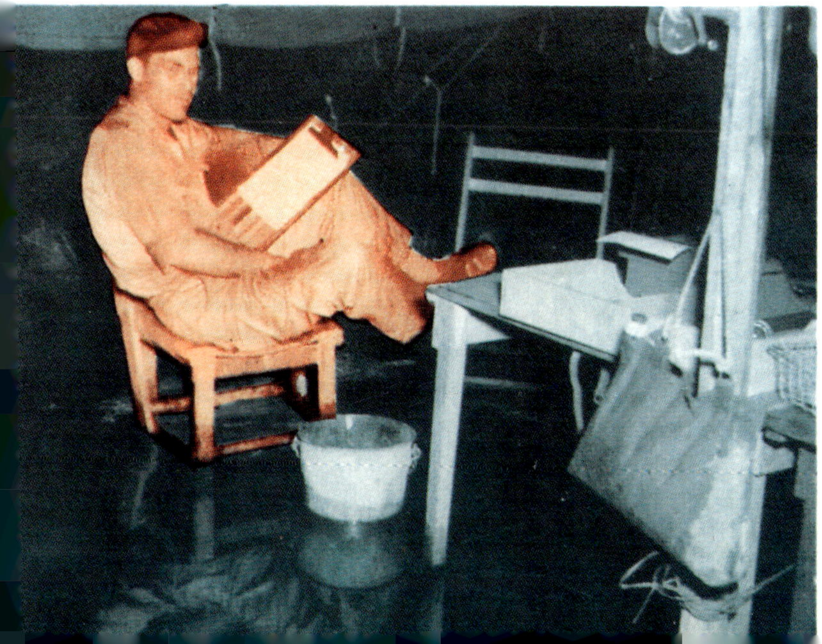

LEFT: When those cursed Guinea thunderstorms left our tents submerged, and shoes floated out to sea? And when you shivered through the night in soaked blankets?

RIGHT: When top funny man Bob Hope, after a terrific reception in Australia, came North to clown for us, flew in a Liberator named after him, and obligingly posed for us with a Banzai rag in a Jap jeep?

BEST DAMN PLANE PATCHERS IN THE WORLD . .

ABOVE: Work-site of the WOODLINGS, a compact field "bomber hospital" where ailing Liberators get put back on their wheels.

ABOVE: *The JOLLY ROGERS plane on the WOODLINGS' sign speaks eloquently of the close co-operation and friendship between the two veteran units.*

LEFT: *Major Francis E. Woodling, who's best known to his men bare-chested, with a turned-up mechanic's cap concealing his gold leaf. His motto: "Work!"*

RIGHT: Welding Shop foreman, getting in a few licks with his acetylene torch. Most of these boys were work-trained overseas.

LEFT: *Engine Shop. Freshly uncrated, right from the States, these high-h.p. jobs are re-checked and tested before going into action.*

"WHAT the hell good is an airplane that won't fly?" With that hard-boiled slogan, Major Francis E. Woodling and his veteran aircraft service unit have doctored ailing JOLLY ROGERS' B-24's ever since February, 1942. At one time the WOODLINGS took care of every combat bomber and fighter outfit flying in the Southwest Pacific. There was no one else around to do it.

The WOODLINGS were the very first Air Corps Service unit to go north of Townsville, Australia. They spent a year and three months in the jungles of the Northern Territory, then another two years in Guinea.

ABOVE: *A Liberator that's been through the works—but good—gets its horizontal stabiler changed. Notice the size of the tai in proportion to the crew. But it probably looms even larger to the Japs!*

UPPER LEFT: *No stripes on the Sergeant's stripped-for-work arm a he doctors an R-1830 engine. Guinea heat makes bare torso fashionable.*

LOWER LEFT: Chief Aircraft Inspector checks up on a pro repairman.

BELOW: Feathered props on this engine are explained by the fac that this B-24 just returned from a mission. When business i booming, no time is lost in getting the big boys in shape for th next round.

LEFT: *Prop Shop. No fun when these huge bomber props fall on your big toe! When a pilot talks about a "feathered prop," he doesn't mean its weight!*

BELOW: *Radio Shop. As important as any other shop of the* WOODLINGS. *These radios are for air-to-ground communication.*

BOVE: Crew chief at work.

ELOW: Parachute Shop. Packng 'chutes is an arduous, elicate job. These boys take heir responsibilities seriously—ne careless mistake and an irman's life might be on their onsciences. Notice the huge ietal JOLLY ROGERS insignia in he background. Notice also he GI at a sewing machine. Home was never like this!)

LEFT: Tech. Supply. You've got to be tough in this racket, says Lt. Crate. Otherwise they'll talk you out of your underpants.

RIGHT: Dope and Fabric Shop. It's all right when you just have to win your wings, but when you've got to keep repairing 'em . . . !

ABOVE: Headquarters. Looks civilized, but step outside and you'll trip over giant tree-roots and get lost in a tangle of jungle trees.

BELOW: Mess team. Most maligned, most ungrateful job of them all. But these boys look at home on the range.

ABOVE: *Carpentry Shop. Foreman is operating a band-saw which he built from odds-and-ends of junk. Resourcefulness ubber alles!*

BELOW: *Major Woodling takes a look at some work on the line. Line Chief on stand, M/Sgt. Pizzuto, holds Legion of Merit.*

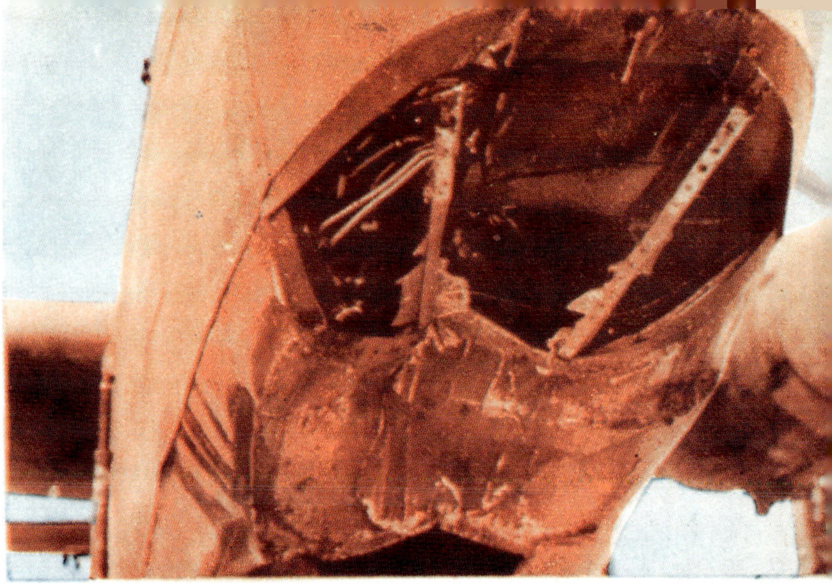

ABOVE: Nothing these boys can't
o. . Here's bomber "CHANGE O'
UCK" getting an operation to
hange her into a transport. They
ven changed her name to "WHITE
ARGO."

ELOW: Accidents will happen.
lo one was hurt in this one.
OODLINGS go to the rescue to get
er up and out of the way.

LEFT: Bombsight Shop. Work as fine and temperamental as the elite of Swiss watch-making. This shop may spell doom or success for a mission.

RIGHT: Machine Shop. In the early days the WOODLINGS, short of supply, practically had to build their own machines out of spare junk.

ABOVE: This is "before." "BLONDE BOMBER" seems to have had a swift kick under the chin. But that's routine to the WOODLINGS, who swiftly . . .

BELOW: . . . fix her up as good as new. Here's the face-lifted "BLONDE BOMBER" with her new chin, and quite snazzy, too.

ABOVE: *That isn't a rock behind the Major—it's an ant hill. One of the rather amazing sights you frequently see down under.*

Maj. General Whitehead congratulates Capt. Jay T. Robbins, top man of the HEADHUNTERS, who had 18 Zeke scalps by last April.

When the Thunderbolts (P-47's) sat overhead, we didn't worry too much about the Zekes. But the Zekes worried . . . plenty!

IGHT: The sight that gladdens the hearts of any bomber crew n mission — P-38's, the speed-demon Lockheed Lightnings.

ELOW: 46 dead Japs and 46 junked Zeros are ccrued to this quintette of fighter Aces. L. to R., Homer (13), Ladd (10), DeGraffenreid (6), Adams (6), Smith Jr. (11).

BEST DAMN TOP

NO heavy bombers ever had finer top-cover than these scrap-hungry fighter pilots gave us. Most of the time we had Yanks for company, sometimes Aussies. But we never expect to see a more beautiful sight for the rest of our lives than those glinting fighter planes weaving a web of air protection around our echelons. Heartfelt thanks, fellas!

A flight of Thunderbolts begins to peel off. And can those babies dive!

Sometimes, when the Japs saw 'em coming, the sons of heaven would retire to another corner of the air and dog-fight among themselves, to give their squint-eyed comrades on the ground the impression of "engaging the enemy."

Sometimes Kittyhawks, sometimes Thunderbolts, sometimes Aircobras, sometimes Lightnings . . . but always the same grim determination — the heavies must get through!

COVER IN THE WORLD . . .

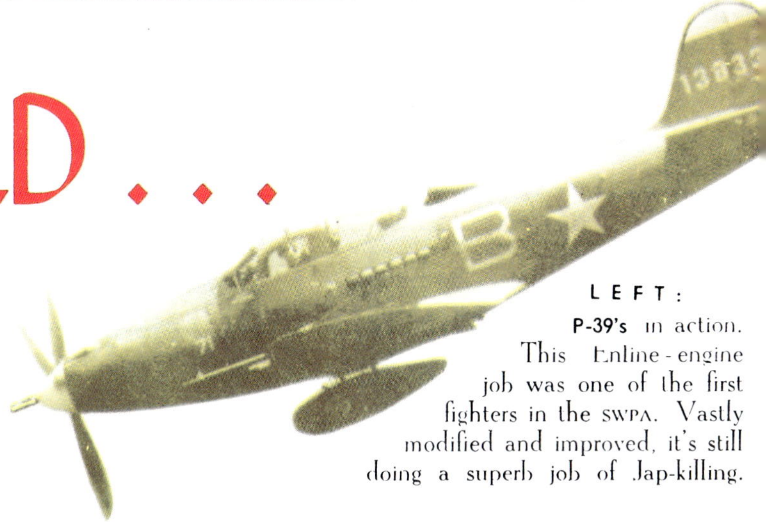

LEFT:

P-39's in action. This Enline - engine job was one of the first fighters in the SWPA. Vastly modified and improved, it's still doing a superb job of Jap-killing.

"No greater glory, than that a man should lay down his life for his brother . . ."

P-39's *lined up for action at an advanced fighter strip.*

A neat piece of work by KEN'S MEN'S outstanding hero, Major Ken McCullar, regrettably lost in action.

YANK FAR EAST, writing about the renowned JOLLY ROGERS-KEN'S MEN feud, said: "So far no one has been tarred and feathered . . . (Both units) have to do a perfect job. If they didn't the rival faction would laugh them right off this beautiful enchanting tropic isle."

Best Damn Rivals in the World . . .

And the Best Damn Feud in the World

EVERYONE in the SWPA recognizes that the JOLLY ROGERS is the "best damn heavy bomber unit in the world." Everyone, naturally, but KEN'S MEN. Alas, we realize how humiliating it must be to belong to the "*second* best damn, etc." We therefore view with compassion the efforts of this otherwise splendid competitor to minimize the glory of the acknowledged kingpin Liberator outfit. That these efforts have included ramming our signs, defiling them, pinching them, swiping our flag, and otherwise indulging in juvenile nose-thumbing, we sadly deplore. Ah, yes, heavy lies the head that wears the crown. But since it is the obvious duty of aerial royalty to "forgive them, for they know not what they do." we hereby make this generous offer to our feuding rivals. If KEN'S MEN will come to us filled with the spirit of brotherly love, we will gladly teach them how to fly, how to hit a target first run over, and how to keep formation. Who knows—perhaps some day a few of KEN'S MEN's best fliers *might* become good enough to win a transfer into the JOLLY ROGERS!

Above is a factual photo of what has been described as KEN'S MEN's first successful mission—a paint bulb smack on the target. At right is the famous pirate flag swiped by certain envious persons,

A famous KEN'S MEN B-24, "Shining Example," gets her name painted on.

TAKE ATABRINE—FOR THAT SCHOOL GIRL COMPLEXION

"We wish to report one Zeke, definite."

"What a Co-pilot!"

One For All
and
All For One!

LIFE MAGAZINE devoted a two-page spread to this dramatic story of a JOLLY ROGERS crew who were forced to bail out in a wild area of Guinea, too rough to land a rescue plane.

RIGHT: Another JR crew that had to hit the silk.

Jolly Rogers RESCUE

LOW: *After being supplied by air for several ys, men on ground signalled they would ave for nearby emergency landing strip at a.m. "T" means "Yes, injured man well ough to be ferried out on light plane."*

WHEN bad weather and engine trouble made the pilot of a JOLLY ROGERS' B-24 order the crew to bail out, all landed safely, although one man had a bad spill. Friendly natives took them to their village, fed and housed them in return for shining gimmicks and smokes. To attract the attention of search planes, they laid out their parachutes in the shape of the JOLLY ROGERS insignia. Eyes for the skull were made by two natives who squatted on the chutes in the appropriate places.

LEFT: *Aussie Moth pilots who flew to rescue*

CIRCLE & ABOVE: Rescued crew and Tiger Moth that flew them out, one at a time.

War Correspondents Praise Jolly Rogers' Ace War Achievements

EVER since the first JOLLY ROGERS insignia was painted on the tail of a Liberator, the famous air pirate outfit has been toasted in printer's ink. When correspondents want to cover a big strike in the SWPA, they usually make a bee-line to the JR camp, to get a ring's-side view with JR pilots. The list of newspapers which have published headline stories on the JOLLY ROGERS is endless. Among the many magazines and syndicate features which have carried long narratives on their exploits are the SATURDAY EVENING POST, with a series of articles by Chuck Rawlings, LIBERTY ("Raid on Rabaul"), YANK FAR EAST, LIFE, AIRCRAFT AGE, PLANE TALK, POST EXCHANGE, UNITED PRESS, ASSOCIATED PRESS, INTERNATIONAL NEWS SERVICE, "BELIEVE IT OR NOT" and Lowell Thomas.

As Brig. General Crabb whimsically observed, folks back home may have gathered the impression that the JOLLY ROGERS is an Air Force in itself. To set *that* misconception straight, the JR's are part of the Fifth Air Force, which is part of the Far East Air Forces. The factor that probably drew more attention to the JOLLY ROGERS than any other was their record in shooting down Zeros. Some envious detractors tried to explain it away by claiming that the JR's flew loose formations, thus inviting enemy attacks. But the truth of the matter is that many of the early JR missions, particularly those of the Asterperious unit, were long and dangerous unescorted strikes. Interception was always heavy . . . but the hot guns of JR crews were more than equal to the challenge.

The JOLLY ROGERS has also been fortunate in its bombardiers. Their bombs have crashed on Nip targets with almost uncanny accuracy, earning many special commendations and awards from Bomber Command. In addition, the JOLLY ROGERS have pioneered in such spectacular feats as introducing "skip-bombing" into Liberator tactics (picture as published in LIFE on Page 28), a dangerous but effective innovation.

Small wonder, then, that among correspondents the JOLLY ROGERS are known as "the best damn *colorful* outfit in the world."

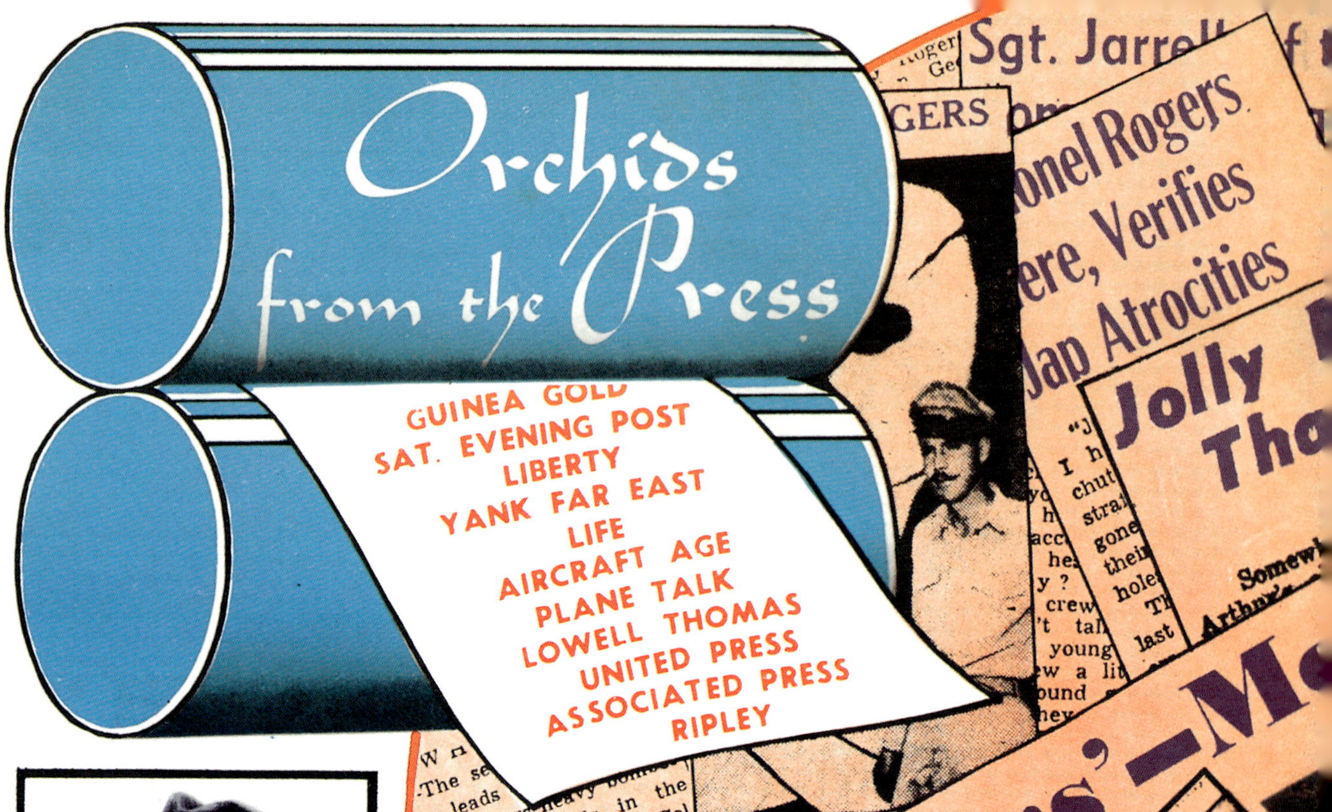

HEADY FAME!

We hope this tribute by a hat manufacturer doesn't swell our heads so's the hat won't fit. Other manufacturers, such as Timkin Roller Bearings, have tied up their salestalks with praise for the JR's.

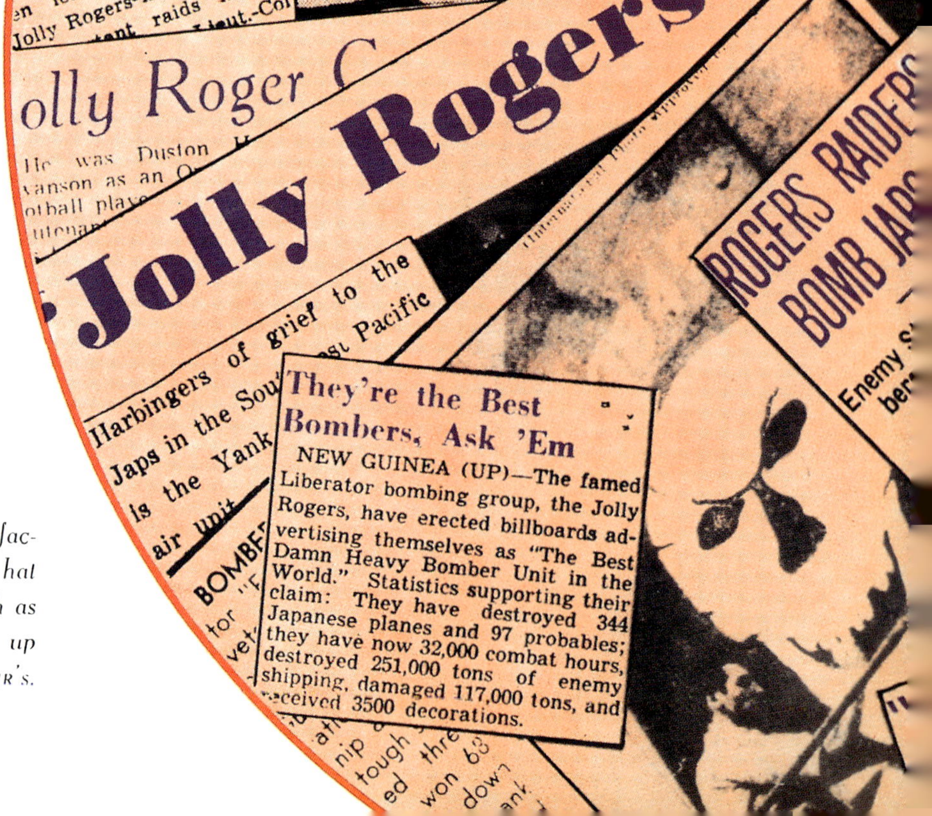

They Say:

"A Liberator formation widely known as the JOLLY ROGERS shot down 39 of the fighters and claimed an additional 10 probables. This is regarded as the most amazing performance of heavy bombers against the enemy in the Pacific war. . . ."

"Famous JOLLY ROGERS unit, whose dreaded insignia of a grinning skull and crossed bones is known and feared by all Jap airmen in the South Pacific. . . ."

Bulletin board at JOLLY ROGERS Headquarters.

JR'S NAB NIPS IN JUNGLE

Not satisfied with liquidating the Sons out of heaven, the JOLLY ROGERS have turned Infantry to dig 'em out of the ground. Well, at least two JR's did recently. It all began when a Jap sneaked into the JOLLY ROGERS camp area, and tried to toss a grenade at Lt. Col. Banks. Scared off by Captain Smith, he took to the hills. Next day S/Sgt. George Mathers, waist gunner, and Cpl. Clarence Mitchell, ordnance man, went a-huntin'.

Along a coral path they spotted several newly-opened cans, and drew their .45's. As they made a sharp turn, they suddenly saw them. "Nips!" yelled Mathers. The JR's motioned for the Japs to throw up their hands. One tried to break away through the underbrush. Mitchell fired three rounds. The Jap fell.

The second Nip, without delay, put his hands up and pleaded, "No shoot me. Father from Chicago." His captors loaded him in their truck. On the way back the prisoner, whose English left much to be desired, declared, "Father from Chicago, mother Tokyo." When they passed a Yank cemetery, scene of recent bitter fighting, the Nip said, "Velly solly. America win war. No want Army."

Eyeing the white crosses angrily, Mathers said, "Yeah, we're very sorry, too, you yella basket. Velly solly we no liquidate you, too!"

Now all that has to happen is for our JOLLY ROGERS crash boat to sink a Nip cruiser, and we'll amend our motto to read: "Best Damn Heavy Bomber Unit in the World—On Land, in the Air, and on the Sea!"

HIGHLIGHTS in the HEADLINES

Allied Hdq. Communique, Oct. 24, 1943 (AP)

"The heaviest bombing of the New Guinea campaign, administered by America's flying 'JOLLY ROGERS' on Japanese troops trying to escape entrapment above Finschhafen, paved the way today for an expected Australian move designed to wipe out the Japanese and consolidate the allied hold on Huon Peninsula. . . . The attack blew up 25 to 28 buildings and 'just blew that place to hell'."

Saturday Evening Post article; Jan. 8, 1944
"Buzzin' Johnny Gets His Medal" by Chuck Rawlings

"The Liberator unit Colonel Rogers has brought across the Pacific bears a number close to 100 and he has made it one of the crack heavy units of the world. Its gunnery and its bombing are bywords in the Pacific, and for a full year it has fought ack-ack and Zero and the champion enemy of them all, New Guinea's terrifying turbulence, the cumulus weather. It has three long files—dead men, missions and honors."

Lowell Thomas Broadcast, March 20, 1944

"They are proud of themselves and they don't mind letting the world know it. In fact, they have built billboards in New Guinea, advertising themselves as the 'best so-and-so' heavy bombing unit in the world.' Their claim seems pretty good. In addition to the planes they have destroyed, they have sunk more than 260,000 tons of enemy shipping, and damaged 117,000 more. They have to their credit a total of more than 32,000 combat hours, flying an average of three missions a week, two a day when necessary."

"Wing Tips," Raleigh, N.C. newspaper column

"So much has been written about Colonel Arthur Rogers (and his outfit) that we know there is little we can add. Newspapers and national magazines have carried many tales of his heroic work in the Pacific war zone."

Associated Press dispatch, October 12, 1943

"Members of JOLLY ROGERS units called today's exhibition of bombing 'Dunmore's Glory Run,' because the bombardier already is leading the league out here with six definite Jap ships sunk. Whether he got two or four today, his eight mile run over the target of four destroyers and one destroyer tender makes him still the champ."

Post Exchange Magazine, April, 1944

"The most famous insignia in Southwest Pacific skies is a huge, leering skull under which are two crossed bombs. The bombers on whose twin tails they are painted are the deadly Liberators belonging to the famous modern pirates of the sky, the JOLLY ROGERS."

Ripley's "Believe It Or Not"

"Lost 141 days! Staff Sergeant Grady Gaston (of the JOLLY ROGERS) s vived a forced landing of his Liberator bomber in Northern Australia a wandered 141 days in the wilds before being rescued. Three of companions perished—he existed on snakes, fish and crocodiles—a lost 60 pounds."

Plane Talk Magazine, May, 1944
Article, "Portrait of a Liberator"

"He has led the JOLLY ROGERS on most of the exciting SWPA stri which are now part of history."

Liberty Magazine, August 5, 1944
Article, "Raid on Rabaul"

"His bomb unit has been nicknamed the JOLLY ROGERS and they h made headline history."

Aircraft Age article, "All-American Bomber Team"

"Certainly if any heavy bomber unit deserves the right to nominate All-American Bomber Team, that right belongs to the famous JC ROGERS."

Yank Far East, January 7, 1943
Lead article, "Jolly Roger"

"Liberators of the AAF's leading bomber outfit wear a grinning s and crossed bombs, while modern Buccaneers gather loot in destro Jap ships and planes. . . . It is the insignia of the JOLLY ROGERS, most famous trademark in this theatre of war."

STOP PRESS

As this portion of the book goes to press, word comes of Fift Air Force attacks against Balikpapan, Borneo. . . . JOLLY ROGER led the heavies over Balikpapan twice out of three attacks in fortnight, completely destroyed targets of urgent importance, sho down 22 more Zeros, probably destroyed another 12, damaged 1 . . . This brings JR Zero tally to 396 destroyed, 132 probable 104 damaged. General MacArthur wired General Kenney "BALIKPAPAN STRIKE WAS MAGNIFICENT PI CONVEY MY SINCEREST COMMENDATION TO AL CONCERNED."

And Brother, We've Just Begun to Fight!

Somerville

Brown

Josket

Bird

Porter

Horne

Last but not Least

Lt. Col. Wilson H. Banks

Keefe

AUTOGRAPHS

For censorship reasons, only signatures *without* messages may be written here if book is intended for mailing.

The End

PAPPYS PASSION
THE BUTCHER BOX
'PLUTO'
LIBERTY BELLE
THE LEMON
SCORPION
The CORAL QUEEN
How'm-I-Doin'
DINKY
ASTERPERIOUS SPECIAL
The Duchess of Paducah
ROARIN' ROSIE
MR.
TWIN NIFTY'S
The NIPPER
LOUISIANA LULLABY
THE STRIP POLKA